The Doctor's Touch . . .

"Come in and get it over with," Joshua called.

He'd pulled up the top sheet until it covered him from head to toe, and shut the drapes so that only a sliver of light peeked through.

Kristie flipped on the light as she entered the room.

"Turn off the damn light," Joshua shouted.

"Don't be ridiculous," Kristie said. "Do you think you're the first male body I've—" she whipped back the sheet, swallowed and finished weakly "—seen?"

Joshua heard the pause; he glanced over his shoulder and saw her blush. *She isn't totally immune to me, either*, he realized. That realization fanned the flames of his imagination. He smothered a low groan with the pillow.

The tube of ointment Kristie had been rolling between her hands to warm it was growing increasingly slippery from the dampness of her palms. She reminded herself sternly that Joshua Hayden was a patient in need of a rubdown for muscular pain. She couldn't, *wouldn't* think of him as a man.

Dear Reader:

Happy Holidays from all of us at Silhouette Books. And since it *is* the holiday season, we've planned an extra special month at Silhouette Desire. Think of it as our present to you, the readers.

To start with, we have December's *Man of the Month*, who comes in the tantalizing form of Tad Jackson in Ann Major's *Wilderness Child*. This book ties into the Children of Destiny series, but Tad's story also stands on its own. Believe me, Tad's a man you'd *love* to find under your Christmas tree.

And what would December be without a Christmas book? We have a terrific one—*Christmas Stranger* by Joan Hohl. After you've read it, I'm sure you'll understand why I say this is a truly timeless love story.

Next, don't miss book one of Celeste Hamilton's trilogy, Aunt Eugenia's Treasures. *The Diamond's Sparkle* is just the first of three priceless love stories. Look for *Ruby Fire* and *Hidden Pearl* in February and April of 1990.

Finally, some wonderful news: the *Man of the Month* will be continued through 1990! We just couldn't resist bringing you one more year of these stunning men. In the upcoming months you'll be seeing brand-new *Man of the Month* books by Elizabeth Lowell, Annette Broadrick and Diana Palmer—just to name a few. Barbara Boswell will make her Silhouette Desire debut with her man. I'll be keeping you updated....

Before I go, I want to wish all of our readers a very Happy Holiday. See you next year!

Lucia Macro
Senior Editor

JO ANN ALGERMISSEN

BEDSIDE MANNER

SILHOUETTE *Desire*

Published by Silhouette Books New York

America's Publisher of Contemporary Romance

SILHOUETTE BOOKS
300 East 42nd St., New York, N.Y. 10017

Copyright © 1989 by Jo Ann Algermissen

ISBN: 0-373-05539-0

First Silhouette Books printing December 1989

Printed in the U.S.A.

JO ANN ALGERMISSEN

lives near the Atlantic Ocean, where she spends hours daydreaming to her heart's content. She remembers that as a youngster, she always had "daydreams in class" written on every report card. But she also follows the writer's creed: write what you know about. After twenty-five years of marriage, she has experienced love—how it is, how it can be and how it ought to be. Mrs. Algermissen has also written under a romanticized version of her maiden name, Anna Hudson.

One

___

"Twitch his nose harder," Kristie ordered, dabbing antiseptic ointment liberally on Feisty's scratches and scrapes. She shifted to the right of the horse's back leg. "Dusty, I'm going to have a hoofprint on my chest if you don't wake up!"

Dusty, who had been distracted momentarily by the swirl of white sand trailing behind a black Cherokee driving down the lane, grumbled at the woman hunched beside the stallion. "Some bedside manner you've got, Kristie Fairbanks. I'll bet you use one of these contraptions on your patients' noses instead of puttin' them to sleep."

Kristie wiped the perspiration from her brow with the sleeve of her shirt, leaving a brown streak of medicine slashing from the widow's peak of her blond hair to the dimple in her left cheek. Finished ministering to the barbed-wire cut, she lowered Feisty's hoof to the packed sand and sent Dusty a cocky grin.

"Only on cantankerous, hardheaded mules like you," she said good-naturedly.

Her hands moved to the small of her back as she stretched to straighten out the kinks in her spine and waited for Dusty's barbed retort. Kristie was certain Dusty's second love was bickering, second only to Maude—his wife and the Fairbanks' housekeeper. She and Dusty had been jawboning each other from the first time he'd changed her diaper and she'd let out a howl of protest. She jokingly blamed her short stature on Dusty's constantly whittling her down to size.

"Oh, yeah?" His shaggy mustache twitched downward, signaling a hit, but he still got in a last word. "Guess that's why you get along better with four-legged stallions than the two-legged variety, huh?"

Kristie groaned, then reached up and tweaked his mustache. "You're beating a dead horse, Dusty! I'm the first person to admit that becoming a 'domestic goddess' isn't my top priority."

"Domestic goddess, my hind leg!" He batted at her fingers before they could nab his cheek. "The word you're searching for is *housewife*! You're almost thirty, but there are still some words I can't teach you to say, huh?"

Feisty nickered and pawed the ground impatiently, as though he were anxious to hear her reply.

"Nope." Grinning, she reached into the pocket of her jeans for a sugar cube. Unlike a man, she silently mused, a stallion was content with an occasional sweet treat. A man wouldn't settle for anything less than her undivided attention, and that was something she wasn't sure she wanted.

"You know you'd be better off staying here, taking care of your dad, instead of running between Ocala and Orlando like a chicken with your head cut off. I've been telling your dad ever since he had his heart attack that if he had an ounce of smarts he'd hire somebody to manage those emergency care centers he owns, just like he hired me to run things around here."

Fairly certain that Dusty was just tweaking her nose to get a sassy reply, Kristie covered up her hurt by pretending to inspect Feisty's ears. Dusty would tease her mercilessly if he realized how sensitive she was about her father hiring outside help to run the business end of the clinics.

Lately Carlton had been dropping unsubtle hints about "easing the burden from her shoulders." Translated that meant "Run along and play while I find someone to do the men's work."

"Men's work," Kristie muttered. She'd thought getting her medical degree would earn her father's love and respect. It hadn't. She'd thought taking over the running of the clinics after her father's heart attack would earn her his gratitude. It hadn't. Her efforts to prove herself competent, efficient and productive had earned her nothing but bewildered glances from him.

Obviously she'd thought wrong.

Sure, he'd put her name on the corporate papers as minority stockholder while he'd been hospitalized, but once he'd started to recover he'd begun to resent her competence as a doctor and as an administrator. Carlton alternated between wanting her to be a little girl who kept her mouth shut and stayed out of trouble, and wanting her to be a woman like her deceased mother, sweet and docile.

Neither role suited Kristie.

Maybe some of Dusty's ornery cussedness had rubbed off on her. Stubbornly she continued to try to prove to Carlton that a woman could be more than a decorative sugary confection. A real woman had substance; she could bear the brunt of responsibility on her shoulders as easily as a man.

Dusty nodded towards the Cherokee, which was pulling up in front of the house. This timely arrival gave him the ammunition he needed to win the skirmish. "Maybe somebody around here is smart enough to listen to an old cowpoke. That's the same fella I saw Doc Fairbanks talking to a couple of weeks ago."

He chuckled triumphantly when Kristie pivoted on one foot and turned to face the house. Hands on her hips, she narrowed her eyes as she glared at the Jeep.

"Dad wouldn't make a decision to hire someone for the centers without consulting me."

Dusty's hoot of laughter earned him a dirty look. "Sayin' it don't make it true," he pointed out.

Kristie scowled. She might be a full partner in the Fairbanks Care Centers, Inc., but she knew her father was perfectly capable of making important decisions without consulting her. Much to her chagrin, he did it frequently. She still had little voice in the overall management of the company.

Dusty's chuckles were salt on an open wound. She countered, "This man doesn't look like a city slicker. Maybe Dad's found somebody to help you train the horses."

Dusty rocked back on his heels when he heard this below-the-belt remark. His hand shot forward and grabbed Kristie's shoulder. "You can't let some young whippersnapper get my job! You wouldn't have nobody to fight with."

Kristie felt a sharp stab of remorse. Dusty might hurt her sometimes, but she hadn't realized he was insecure about his job. She thought he knew she wouldn't let her father put him out to pasture any more than she'd let a stranger be hired to replace her.

"I was kidding, Dusty. We wouldn't know what to do around here without you." Feeling doubly rotten because his fears were the same as her own, she reassured, "The stranger is carrying a briefcase, not a saddle. He's probably a detail man from a pharmaceutical company trying to sell a new line of medicine."

Slightly mollified, Dusty gave her a grin. "You better get on out of here and find out what the Doc is up to—just in case. I'll put Feisty back in his stall and finish up the chores."

Nodding, she hurried toward the front drive. She was halfway to the corral fence when Dusty shouted, "You'd better wipe the dirt off your face!"

Automatically she swiped ineffectually at her cheeks with her clean sleeve; then she realized that Dusty was talking about the Mercurochrome ointment on her face. It would take more than a swipe to remove that.

Knowing her father's dislike of untidy females, Kristie considered taking a quick shower before presenting herself, but her curiosity got the better of her.

What the heck, she reasoned. So what if her father would give first aid to a horse without mussing his pristine white medical jacket. She couldn't and he knew it. He'd disapprove of her meeting a stranger looking anything less than the lady of the manor, but she didn't have to dress up to say no to a pharmaceutical salesman. It wasn't as if there were any expected guests.

"Kristine! Come meet our guests!" her father called. His voice was deceptively warm, considering the frigid blueness of his eyes as they perused the straggling wisps of hair that had come loose from her ponytail and the smudges on her face.

"Guests?"

Exasperated by the sudden news of guests so near the dinner hour, Kristie glanced in the direction of the dusty vehicle, her eyes echoing the frostiness in her father's. The Jeep appeared to be empty. Her brows drew together and she turned back to her father again. He was resting his hand amiably on the muscular shoulder of a stranger.

"My son is still in the Cherokee," the stranger volunteered.

Her eyes rounded in surprise. She'd heard an amused tone in his voice. The man's eyes were dancing with laughter, but his lips were taut.

Kristine hated contradictions. A man with laughter in his voice shouldn't be scowling like a schoolmaster ready to administer the rod to the backside of a mischievous student.

"Joshua Hayden, meet my daughter, Kristine," Carlton said.

As her eyes moved from the cleft in the stranger's chin to the hand extended toward her, she refused to mask her own amusement. From the collar of his starched cotton shirt to the crease in his brand-new Levi's and right down to the shiny boots on his feet, his clothes shouted "Dude!" If Dusty had seen Joshua Hayden up close he'd have known he didn't have to worry about his job. This man probably couldn't tell a twitch from a cattle prod.

"Kristine." Joshua silently estimated her age. Thirteen, maybe fourteen. Someone to keep Drew out of trouble while he worked. Carlton hadn't mentioned having two daughters, but this obviously wasn't the daughter he'd been warned about. The older daughter knew he was coming; Carlton had fervently promised to consult with his partner before Joshua arrived.

His estimate of her age changed when he saw the poised manner in which she shook hands. He stepped back and looked beneath the streak of dirt marring the face which was devoid of makeup.

Maybe she's sixteen, he thought.

"Mr. Hayden." Kristie's polite smile widened as she watched the play of emotions flickering across Joshua Hayden's face. Unless she was badly mistaken, he'd equated her height with her age...not an uncommon occurrence. In her professional dealings with male doctors, she'd often found it advantageous to let them underestimate her. Penicillin came in small packages, and yet it was a wonder drug. She promised herself that before the evening was over Joshua Hayden would consider her a wonder, too.

Joshua glanced questioningly at Carlton.

The older man's downcast eyes confirmed his suspicions: one, this woman was closer to his own age than to his son's, and that meant she must be Carlton's only daughter; two, Carlton hadn't informed her of his decision to hire a business consultant. What should have been a simple business arrangement was developing complications.

"Dr. Kristine Fairbanks," Carlton said, his face turning a guilty shade of red. "She looks young for her age."

Not young enough to suit you, Kristie thought, irritated. "Father, if you excuse me, I'll inform Maude that we'll be having guests for dinner. I'm certain she can stretch the tuna fish casserole to accommodate them."

"Tuna fish?" she heard through the open window of the Cherokee. "Blecch."

"Drew!" Joshua said firmly, the laughter in his eyes replaced by wariness. "Do you need assistance getting out of the car?"

Kristie cringed. Her father had used that same tone of voice with her throughout her teenage years. Instantly she sympathized with the youngster in the Jeep. She shot Joshua Hayden a quelling glare.

The passenger door creaked as it opened. One dirty tennis shoe, then another, landed reluctantly on the paved driveway. The door slammed shut.

Kristie scrutinized Drew's shabby jeans and surfer's T-shirt as carefully as she had measured Joshua's new clothing. Physically there was a family resemblance. Both man and boy were tall, with dark hair and dark eyes. She glanced from the mulish thrust of Drew's rounded chin to the determined hardness of Joshua's jaw. The fist knotted at the boy's side was a smaller version of the doubled fingers shoved into the pockets of the man's jeans.

At that point, the resemblance ceased to exist. Whereas the father's cool reserve masked his emotions, the boy's stance fairly shrieked defiance. The dark hatred gleaming in the son's eyes was met by the thinly veiled anger glittering in the father's.

From her own rebellious teenage years Kristie remembered the curled upper lip, the wad of gum, the hips thrust aggressively forward. This young man had a chip on his shoulder, and for some unknown reason he was openly daring his father to knock it off.

"Fine-looking young man," Carlton said, much to Kristie's surprise. "One day he'll be a son you'll be proud of."

Not any day in the near future, Kristie thought, begrudging the boy the undeserved compliment. She glanced down at her shirt and slacks. Compared to Drew's sloppy outfit, her stable-stained clothing was almost immaculate. Carlton would have died of embarrassment if she'd ever climbed out of a car looking like a beach bum.

"Drew..." Joshua said, a warning chill in his voice that hovered at the freezing level, "come and meet the Fairbankses."

Drew shot his father a go-straight-to-hell look, but he reluctantly stuck out a hand in the older man's direction. "Nice to meet you, sir," he mumbled.

Carlton smiled. "You'll enjoy living in Florida. We're less than an hour from the beaches, and about the same distance from Disney World and Epcot."

"Kid stuff," Drew said scornfully. His hostile eyes darted to his father's face. With a wealth of animosity in his voice, he snarled, "I'd rather be in Boston."

And Kristie was sure he added silently, "Than anywhere with him."

Carlton sent an appealing look at Kristie. She shrugged one shoulder. If her father's award-winning bedside manner couldn't charm Drew, she wasn't about to volunteer assistance. These were his guests, not hers. Next time Carlton would think twice before inviting guests without informing her.

"Uh, Kristie, why don't you take this fine young man down to the stables and introduce him around while

Joshua and I finalize a couple of business matters.
You'd like that, Drew, wouldn't you?''

I wouldn't, Kristie mutely responded. Joshua Hayden was obviously neither pharmaceutical salesman nor
horse trainer. Whatever business her father had to discuss with the stranger, she wanted to add her two cents'
worth. If necessary, she wanted to be in a position to
throw the weight of her fifty percent of the company's
stock to squelch the bargain. What she didn't want to
do was play nursemaid to a cantankerous kid while the
two men conducted business.

Unfortunately for Kristie, Drew's whole counte-
nance changed from sullen resentment to exuberant
anticipation faster than she could snap her fingers.
''Horses? Can I ride one?''

''No,'' Joshua interjected, explaining, ''The closest
Drew has been to a horse is seeing one on television.''

''Gimme a break, Joshua, would you?''

Joshua? Kristie took another hard look at the man
towering over her. She hadn't called her father by his
given name until she'd graduated from medical school!

Someone had to pull the reins on this kid's behavior
or he'd be a pint-size dictator before he reached driving
age. Carlton's bedside manner had failed; Joshua's cold
disapproval had failed. What this kid needed was the
kind of bare-knuckled shock treatment Dusty had given
her.

''Where would you like your break?'' Kristie asked
sweetly. ''In the arm? The leg? Or how about somewhere in the region of your posterior?''

She'd been silent so long that Drew's jaw dropped at
her audacity, but then a full-fledged grin curved his lips.
His finger rose and pointed in her direction. ''You I'm
gonna like.''

"He would," Joshua muttered, none too happy with his son's choice of friends. He was starting to get the feeling that once he put his name on the dotted line of the contract in his briefcase Kristie would consider him a sworn enemy. He'd have enough trouble convincing Kristie he was the best thing that could have happened to Fairbanks Care Centers and helping Drew adjust to being with him without Drew and Kristie forming an alliance against him.

"I beg your pardon, Mr. Hayden?"

"He could," Joshua said smoothly. "Ride, I mean. Later. I'll hire someone to give him lessons while we're staying here."

Kristie's head snapped toward her father. Dinner guests and house guests were horses of a different color! Now she was certain her father was up to something.

"They're staying at the cottage near the lake," Carlton explained with a wary shrug of his shoulders.

"No one can stay there," Kristie blurted out.

"We don't mind roughing it. We don't want to impose on you. We'll manage, thank you."

"You and the gators, rats and moccasins have something in common?" she inquired hotly. "You'll be sharing your bed with them."

Carlton beamed. "See? I told you she'd insist on your staying in the main house."

Kristie knew exactly how the big, wide, grinning jaws of an alligator felt when they were snapped shut by the heel of a man's hand. Like it or not, she'd opened her big mouth and trapped herself.

"I'll get the guest suite ready," she said grudgingly. That wouldn't take long, and then she'd hotfoot it to the office and find out what the hell her father was up to.

"No, no," Carlton protested. "That won't be necessary. You just run along with Drew down to the stables. I told Maude to prepare the rooms a few minutes ago."

Kristie opened her mouth, but then she saw a flicker of apprehensiveness in Joshua's eyes and shut it again. She wouldn't disgrace herself by ranting and raving like a demented fool. She'd be a lady if it killed her—and it damn well might!

"Come on, Drew," she said briskly. "Let's run along to the stables." *Like obedient little children,* she fumed silently.

Shoulders straight, chin raised, she sashayed out of the front yard with her dignity intact. Drew shuffled along after her, dragging his feet, slouching his shoulders, shifting his wad of bubble gum from one side of his mouth to the other.

"Straighten up," she told him out of the side of her mouth. "And spit out that bubble gum. With your feet scuffing in the sand and your gum popping in your mouth you sound like a tap dancer at a Fourth of July fireworks display! You'll frighten the horses and make them stampede!"

"Oh, yeah?" Drew grinned. "That'd be awesome, huh? I could stampede 'em right through the house and spoil my old man's business meeting. He wouldn't get the job...you'd be rid of us...and I could go back to Boston, where I belong. Awesome!"

Kristie was tempted to tell him to chew faster, harder, if he could guarantee those results.

"What's in Boston?" she asked, slowing down her pace as they neared the corral.

"Not what—who."

"Your mother?"

Kristie bit her lower lip. She had no right to pump Joshua Hayden's son for personal information that was none of her business. Whether Joshua was separated or divorced would have little effect on his business with Carlton. Personally, she didn't care if the man had ten wives in five different states. He was as handsome as sin; he probably did have a nurse in every ward.

"Nope. My grandparents." Drew's chin wobbled and his voice grew hushed. "My mother is dead."

Kristie glanced sideways at him, regretting that she had obviously stirred the boy's grief. "I'm sorry. I know what it's like to be a kid without a mother. My mother passed away when I was about your age."

"Yeah, but you get along with your father. I hate mine."

She opened the corral gate and paused, leaning against the cedar gatepost. She knew little of the circumstances surrounding the boy's hatred of his father, but personal experience had taught her that hating him would only cause the boy more grief. For the youngster's sake, she had to say something constructive, something wise, something that would help him.

"Hating your dad won't bring your mother back" was the best she could think of on a moment's notice.

"No, it won't." Drew stepped into the corral and gave Kristie a hard look. She was barely two or three inches taller than he, and that made it far less intimidating than looking up at his father. He removed the pink wad from his mouth, tossed it next to the fence and raked sand over it with the side of his Reebok. "But it makes him miserable—just like he makes other people miserable. You're gonna hate him, too, before long."

"Why should I hate him?" Her heart fluttered with apprehension. "We've just met."

"Yeah, well, some people you can learn to hate real quick. Joshua is one of them." Drew folded his arms across his chest and kicked at an imaginary pebble. "I overheard him talking on the telephone to your dad before we drove here."

Don't pry, a small voice silently warned Kristie. She felt sorry for Drew, and she wasn't particularly kindly disposed toward his father, but she didn't want to be put in the position of taking sides. She knew that if Drew confided information to her as a means of sealing their friendship he'd expect her to side with him in his private war with his father.

Uh-uh, she decided. She was too old to allow Drew to manipulate her into a compromising position. Any battles she had to fight with Joshua Hayden wouldn't be muddied by his son.

"Ever seen a newborn filly?" she asked, trying to change the subject.

"No." Torn between the desire to see the horse and the desire to blacken his father's character, Drew glanced from her face to the barn and then back to the house. "Don't you want to know what's going on in there?"

"Not particularly," she said. Then, wanting to stay a little closer to the truth, she added, "I can wait."

"Well, just be careful. When Joshua starts making noises about how 'this is for your own good,' that's when you know he's about to shove a bitter pill down your throat."

Kristie grinned. "I'll remember that sage advice, Drew. Just for the record, how old are you?"

"Eleven and three-quarters. I'll be twelve in a couple of months."

"Mmm. That close to being ancient, huh?" she said teasingly, remembering how she had always counted the days until her birthdays. Now she was too close to thirty to want to wish the days away.

"How old are you?"

"Four hundred and fifty-two."

Drew grinned. "You're almost as old as Joshua.

"But a whole lot smarter?" I hope, she added silently.

"Grandfather says I'm smart for my age," he boasted. When he saw that bragging didn't impress Kristie, he added, "Grandmother says he can't tell the difference between smart and smart aleck."

Straightening, Kristie put one arm around Drew's thin shoulders and squeezed lightly. He could be utterly charming when he uncurled his lip and let his smile reach his eyes. She was mildly surprised when he circled her waist with his arms and gave her a quick hug.

"Maybe they're both right. C'mon, Drew, let's take a tour of the barn, and then I'll race you back to the kitchen for some of Maude's chocolate chip cookies and milk."

Joshua, standing at the window, saw the woman-child spontaneously hug his son and saw Drew's reaction. In the five weeks that he'd had custody of Drew the boy had kept him at arm's distance. How had Kristine broken through the barriers Drew had erected? Just once he'd like to see the boy smile at him the way he was beaming at her.

"You didn't tell her about our agreement, did you?" Joshua inquired, turning back to Carlton, who was signing triplicate copies of their agreement.

"I decided to let you break it to her gently once it's a fait accompli." Carlton signed the last page and dropped his pen on the desktop. One look at Joshua's raised eyebrow and he had second thoughts about his reply. "I know I promised to hash this out with her before you arrived. I've started to tell her a dozen times, but—" He shook his silver-gray head regretfully, plowing his fingers through the sparse hairs on his crown. "We talk, but we don't communicate. I decided it would be better if a complete stranger told her."

"Me?" Joshua's lip quirked upward momentarily, then settled back into their normal thin line. "I'll be sharing accommodations with the gators, rats and snakes for certain if I tell her you've turned the administrative responsibilities of the centers over to me."

"Worse. She'll probably try to fire you."

Joshua went over to the side of the desk and picked up the contracts. The attorney who'd drawn up the documents had been made aware of the unusual circumstances surrounding the agreement. Joshua turned to the second page and scanned the paragraph headed Termination of Agreement.

"According to section 3, paragraph five, I can't be fired unless the yearly profits drop by twenty percent."

"You know that, and I know that, but she doesn't." Carlton rubbed the front of his shirt, directly over his heart. "Believe me, if I'd realized making her an equal stockholder in the corporation entitled her to make decisions after I recuperated I'd have had second thoughts before doing it."

"She's your only child." No, woman, Joshua thought, silently correcting himself.

Leaning back in his leather-upholstered swivel chair and looking directly into Joshua's face, Carlton replied, "True. Too true. Can you explain to me how a woman who looks so much like her mother can act so much like me? It's—unfeminine! Gloria, her mother, was perfectly content spending the money I earned without tallying up the daily receipts and questioning my expenditures."

Experience had taught Joshua to listen with more than his ears, and he could tell that Carlton was like many middle-aged men he'd known who'd founded their own businesses—reluctant to relinquish any responsibilities to his offspring. He saw Kristie's wish to examine his books as an infringement of his authority.

Typical of a family business, Joshua mused.

"There's been many a time I've wished I'd just opened an office in the back of my house. Let me assure you, when I started out in medicine I planned on operating on people. I wound up operating five clinics."

"Why did you expand?"

Carlton glanced up at the rows of medical books lining the shelves in the office as he considered Joshua's question. His reply was brutally frank. "Need and greed are the criteria to succeed. Clinics were needed, and I must have been greedy enough to open them, although back then I thought I was being altruistic." He shrugged, as though his pat answer weren't completely truthful. "Hell, I don't know why I opened those clinics. They just . . . happened. But there is one thing I've learned . . . I'm a doctor, not a businessman. And Kristine is a doctor. She isn't any more adept in business matters than I am."

In fairness to Kristine, Joshua felt obligated to reply. "But you did need her help during your recovery."

"I won't argue with facts. I needed her and she was there. What I've never understood is *why* she's there. Why would a woman insist on working fourteen hours a day, six days a week, when she doesn't have to work at all? Haven't I worked hard enough for both of us to live comfortably?" He tapped his chest and added wryly, "Damn right I have. And I've had a heart attack to prove it! Telling her I've hired you would have been enough to bring on the really big one."

Carlton rose and crossed to the window. For a second he watched Kristine and Drew leading Lazy Bones around the corral. He turned to Joshua. "So I'm going to let you tell her about your new job."

"I could refuse."

Joshua's dark eyes met Carlton's without flinching, but both of them knew he was bluffing.

A month ago he'd resigned from his post as administrator of a major Boston hospital. The hectic pace he'd been living for the past ten years had been too much strain on the relationship he needed to establish between himself and Drew.

To put it mildly, his son resented him. To be more explicit, Drew hated him.

Six months. That was how long the judge had given him to get his problems with Drew straightened out. In October there would be another hearing to determine permanent custody. If he couldn't make a friend of his son by then, there was a strong chance of his losing custody to Drew's maternal grandparents.

He wouldn't let that happen.

The employment contract Joshua held in his hands was a mutually beneficial agreement, with only one drawback—a pint-size, dirty-faced princess who wanted Carlton's crown and scepter.

Carlton called his bluff by silently waiting him out.

"I'll tell her," Joshua finally agreed. "I won't like it, but I'll do it."

Two

―――

Please let me ride him,'' Drew begged. Before Kristie could stop him, he opened the stall where Lazy Bones was contentedly munching on her ration of coastal hay. "He won't hurt me! C'mon, Kristie. *Please!*"

Kristie grinned. She knew something Drew didn't. Lazy Bones was a mare.

"Your father said—"

"He said later." He cast her a boyish grin and stroked the horse's black mane. Kristie's thoughtful hesitation gave him the nerve to twist his father's words. "It is later. He won't care if I just sit on the horse and you lead me around. What can happen?"

"Nothing," Kristie admitted. Three-year-olds had ridden Lazy Bones without difficulty. Granted, she was fifteen hands tall, and she might look intimidating to a greenhorn, but she was gentle. "I'll ask your father for permission during dinner. Okay?"

His lower lip protruding, Drew curled his fingers into the horse's mane as though he wouldn't let go unless lightning struck him. "He'll say no. He doesn't want me to have any fun. He never lets me do what I want to do."

"C'mon, Drew, be reasonable," Kristie said, uncomfortable with the realization that she was repeating something Dusty had often said to her. "He's protective because he loves you. He doesn't want to see you hurt."

"He doesn't love me," Drew told her mulishly. "He got custody of me to spite my grandparents. Grandfather says he's just a damn opportunist, whatever that means. Joshua says he loves me, but it's to fool everybody."

Kristie felt her stomach twist. How often had she said the same to Dusty about Carlton? None of Dusty's homespun words of wisdom had convinced her that her father loved her. She doubted she could say anything to change Drew's mind, either, so she kept silent.

"Joshua wants to have somebody to boss around," Drew muttered. "He never lets me do what I want to do 'cause he's too busy working to watch me. It'll be weeks and weeks before he bothers to get someone to teach me how to ride."

"Dusty can teach you."

"You could teach me, but you won't, 'cause you're scared of him. He's gonna be your boss, and—"

"I beg your pardon? Who says he's going to be my boss?"

"He did. He said he quit his job at the hospital to manage a string of clinics in Florida."

"Wonderful," Kristie said sarcastically, striding toward the rack of bridles. "One short ride."

She knew she was about to make a mistake, but the look of pure joy on Drew's face made the prospect of facing Joshua Hayden's anger worthwhile.

Within minutes she had Lazy Bones saddled and bridled. The last shred of Drew's unhappiness melted as they led the horse into the fenced corral. His dark, worshipful eyes followed every movement she made.

"Your legs are almost as long as mine," she said, reaching down to adjust the stirrups. "One notch ought to do the trick."

"Is he gonna buck?" Drew asked hopefully.

"She, Drew. Lazy Bones is a mare. And no, she isn't going to buck. Whiskey is the horse who has lousy manners around here. Remember him? He's the gelding I told you to stay away from because he bites."

"Yeah."

Kristie smiled, knowing Drew would have agreed to anything she'd said. She snapped the lead rope onto the bridle ring and led Lazy Bones to the mounting block. "You mount a horse from the left side. I'll hold the reins until you're settled. Put your left foot in the stirrup and swing on up there."

Joshua rounded the corner of the house in time to see his son scamper up on the mounting block. His face drained of color. From his protective viewpoint, the horse Drew was about to mount was only inches shorter than Boston's tallest skyscraper.

Damn it! He'd told Kristie not to let Drew ride! The Van Horns would demand Drew back in a minute if the boy had an accident!

His throat worked. "Stop!" he whispered hoarsely. Fear for his son's safety outweighed his common sense and propelled him across the yard and over the cedar fence at full speed.

Perched in the saddle, Drew held on to the saddle horn for dear life. He looked down at Kristie's upturned face. "She's bigger from up here, huh?"

"Let go of the saddle horn and take the reins. Don't worry. I've got the lead rope. Lazy Bones isn't going anywhere." The reassuring words were barely out of her mouth when the mare side-stepped. "Whoa, girl. Easy now. Relax, Drew. Don't squeeze your legs."

"Uh-oh," Drew groaned, when he saw Joshua leap the corral fence. Only the certainty that his father's bark was worse than his bite kept him from digging his heels into the horse's flanks.

"You're doing fine, Drew. Steady, Lazy Bones." The mare shifted her haunches, crowding closer to the block; her front hoof pawed the ground. "Behave!"

"Kristie . . ." The closer his father came, the less certain Drew was about his father's bite. Joshua had never laid a hand on him, but he was beginning to worry about that changing in the immediate future. He kicked his foot from the right stirrup and started to swing his leg back over the horse. "I'm gonna get down."

"Sit still Drew."

"But, Kristie . . ."

"Quiet. Stay in the saddle. She's nervous for some reason. Easy, girl," she crooned. Because she was concentrating on calming Lazy Bones and Drew, she didn't notice the man charging across the corral until a large hand appeared from nowhere and grabbed the reins.

"Just what the hell do you thing you're doing?" Joshua asked through clenched teeth.

She jumped, and the lead rope nearly slithered from her hands. She clutched her fingers together. Now she understood why Lazy Bones had been antsy and why Drew had wanted down.

Spikes of anger were radiating from Joshua.

"Dad, don't be mad at Kristie. It's my fault."

Joshua's head snapped upward. He'd waited for weeks to hear Drew call him *Dad*, to look at him with love shining in his eyes. But the love light was directed toward Kristine, not him.

"Back off, mister," Kristie told him. "You're scaring the horse—not to mention the kid."

Her firm command concealed her shaking insides. The look on Joshua's face gave new meaning to the word *angry*. He plainly wanted to throttle her.

"I'll back off as soon as my son dismounts," he countered, his lips barely moving. "I told you—"

"You said I could ride—later," Drew said, coming to Kristie's defense. "It's later."

"Later than we thought," Kristie muttered under her breath.

She hadn't thought she'd have to face the consequences of her actions until Drew had ridden around the corral safely a couple of times. Then she could have used the fact that Drew had survived unharmed as a defense. With Lazy Bones rolling her eyes and her ears flattened against her neck, she could no longer claim that the horse was perfectly harmless. She expected her to toss her head and bolt for the barn at any moment.

Joshua released his hold on the reins and took three steps backward. He'd been around horses enough to recognize the danger signs. Frustrated by Kristie's having countermanded his order, jealous of Drew's obvious affection for her, he ground his back teeth to keep from taking a verbal swipe at both of them.

"Everything's okay, Lazy Bones." Kristie stroked the mare's neck, soothing her with hand and voice. "Easy, girl, easy."

"I'm mounted. Can I go ahead and ride, Dad? Please?"

The wistfulness Joshua heard in Drew's voice, along with being called *Dad* for the second time, was enough to weaken the hardest of hearts. He wanted to say yes, but he knew that by allowing his son to ride he'd be setting a bad precedent. Drew was a smart kid. It wouldn't take him long to realize that he could wrap his father around his little finger merely by calling him *Dad*.

Joshua shifted his weight from one foot to the other. Consistency, he told himself. Wasn't that the first rule in every parenting book he'd read? Earlier he'd sternly refused Drew's request. He'd be asking for discipline problems if he changed his mind. "No!" he said.

"Please," Kristie said, adding her plea to Drew's. She shot Drew a quelling glance, then held out the lead rope to Joshua and looked him straight in the eye. "You can lead him around the corral if you think it will make it safer for your son."

"He disobeyed me," Joshua told her. His black eyes raked both woman and child. "What happens when Drew gets it into his head to ride alone?"

"I won't. I promise!" Drew crossed his heart and raised his right hand. "Please, Dad?"

Kristine edged closer to Joshua, her eyes gleaming. It was as though the lead rope were the gauntlet she'd always wanted to toss at her father's feet. "He won't want to ride alone if you ride with him, will he?"

"I'll never get to ride," Drew grumbled. "He'll be too busy."

"Will you?" Kristie asked.

Silently Joshua wondered who was about to be led around by the nose—the horse or himself! From the gleam in Kristine's blue eyes, he realized that there was more at stake here than dealing with Drew's flagrant disobedience. He couldn't allow her to believe that she could use his own son as a weapon against him.

"Climb down, son."

Tears welling up in his eyes, Drew covered his hurt by curling his upper lip and snarling, "You said you quit your job at the hospital in Boston so you'd have more time to be with me. Just another one of your lies, huh?"

Before either adult could react, Drew jumped off Lazy Bones from the wrong side and ran toward the house.

Kristie glared at Joshua, then turned on her heel and marched Lazy Bones into the barn to keep from sand-blasting Joshua's tough hide with her tongue.

"While you're silently calling me a cold-hearted son of a bitch, add this reason to your list. Your father asked me to inform you that I've signed a contract to take over the administrative duties of the Fairbanks Care Centers."

Kristie stopped dead in her tracks. He'd done it; her father had carried through with his threat to hire a professional administrator. He didn't think she could handle the job. She blinked to stem the flow of moisture brimming in her eyes.

"Should I clean out my office desk, sir?" she asked snidely. "Starting Monday, will I be receiving my work schedule at the same time the other doctors receive theirs?"

"You could make this a smooth transition."

"The hell I will. You're sadly mistaken if you think you can sneak in here behind my back, cozy up to my father and make a mess out of my life! I'll muck out stalls for a living before I work for you!"

"In that case, you'll have to excuse me. While you're shoveling manure in the barn, I'll go to the house and clean up the mess you've made in there."

"Implying that I've made a mess out of my father's business, too?" she managed to croak. She swallowed hard and fumbled with the lead rope until she had Lazy Bones tied to a stall rail.

Minutes passed, with only the ticking of the clock above the door and the soft nickering of horses breaking the silence. Thinking he'd left, she slowly turned until she faced the wide doorway.

Bronzed by the sunlight outside, Joshua Hayden cast a long, ominous shadow into the barn, invading her childhood sanctuary.

He wasn't feeling ominous; he felt like a callous heel. As he'd crossed the lawn, heading toward the corral, he'd silently rehearsed how he'd gently explain to Kristine why he'd been hired, how they could work together to change the financial picture of the clinics, how she could follow her chosen profession of doctor without being burdened with administrative details. But one glance at Drew sitting astride that mountain-size horse, looking at Kristine as though she'd hung the moon and set the stars just for him, had toppled his good intentions.

A sense of failure engulfed him.

"I could quit," Kristie said, when she realized that Joshua wasn't going to respond to her question. Or fire you, she added silently.

"You could, but you won't."

"What makes you so damn certain I'll stick around?" she snapped, trying to use anger as an antiseptic to heal the damage he'd done to her pride. "You hardly know me."

"It takes stamina and perseverance to get a medical degree."

"Skip the flattery. You're too late to use that approach to win me over."

"I never confuse fact with flattery. You're no quitter, *Dr.* Kristine Fairbanks."

"In that case, your logic contradicts itself," she told him. She moved to Lazy Bones's side, lifted the stirrup and yanked on the cinch belt. "You accept my tenacity as a fact, and yet you think I'll blithely step aside to let you take over a job I'm perfectly capable of doing?"

Joshua stepped from the sunlight into the shadows. The fragrance of sweet-smelling hay, leather and horses assaulted him pleasantly. His eyes adjusted to the cozy dimness as he drew closer to her.

"No. You'll fight. You'll attempt to get rid of me before you seriously consider throwing in the towel. My guess is that you believe the end justifies the means." He placed his hand on the horse's rump. The well-trained Lazy Bones side-stepped until Joshua could easily reach the saddle and remove it from her back. "Where's the tack room?"

Kristie found herself mesmerized by the play of shoulder muscles under his thin cotton shirt. She turned her head, and his shirtsleeve brushed against her bare arm, leaving a sprinkling of goose bumps in its wake. She turned her head aside and rubbed her sensitized skin.

She hadn't asked for his help, she didn't need it, and she didn't want it. But she wasn't about to get into a childish tug-of-war over a twenty-pound saddle just to stop him.

She pointed toward the closed door beside the front entry, grabbed the saddle blanket and led the way. Unsettled by an unwanted awareness of his masculinity, she blustered, "I am a stockholder in the corporation. I could fire you."

"Not according to the contract your father and I signed. You'll have to be content with making my life miserable."

With his hands full, he had to wait for her to open the door. His dark eyes unobtrusively measured her small, slender stature. Tiny, but perfectly proportioned, he mused. He followed her into the little room.

Kristie didn't realize how cramped the tack room was until they were both inside it. Her elbow bumped his; his knee pressed against her thigh. She could feel the warmth of his breath caress the hair on the crown of her head.

She'd been in close quarters with other men without feeling as if she were basking in the sunshine of a man's body heat. She tried to recall anything she'd read in scientific studies that could explain her physical reaction to him. Nothing came to mind, except the whisper of his cotton shirt against the back of her blouse.

She'd just met Joshua Hayden! From the little she knew of him, she had to dislike him. He'd arrived, unannounced, and fobbed Drew off on her while he'd signed an agreement with Carlton to take over part of her job. She certainly had grounds to dislike him!

I do dislike him, she told herself silently in an effort to control the heated awareness that marked every spot he'd touched. There had to be a rational scientific explanation for the blood roaring through her veins. And once she was a safe distance away from him she'd think of them.

She had to get out of the tack room—fast.

"Excuse me," she said, in a whisper that was too breathy for her liking.

He turned sideways to let her scoot through the doorway, but that wasn't a bit of help. The tips of her breasts grew turgid as they brushed against his shirt-front. She glanced upward, expecting to see his lips curved with silent laughter. She'd double up her fist and punch him squarely in the solar plexus if he dared to laugh at her.

Joshua pressed his back against the rough-hewn oak boards of the wall. His lips thinned into a straight line as he strove valiantly to control his own involuntary reaction. Although she was a trained doctor who had to be totally familiar with the male physique, he felt certain she'd be shocked by his arousal.

He sure as hell was!

At thirty-something, he thought he'd left this kind of adolescent reaction to women in the back seat of the Chevy he'd sold over a decade ago.

"Excuse me," he grunted, making for the open space outside the tack room.

Kristie chose precisely the same moment to attempt her escape. Her shoulder bounced off his midsection. Weak in the knees, off balance and in danger of falling, she heard him grunt as she grabbed hold of his belt with one hand. She tried to steady herself on the doorjamb, but her nails raked against the boards, driving a splinter into her index finger. Instantly she drew back her injured hand; her elbow gouged his ribs as her head snapped back and collided with his chin. She tried desperately to regain her balance, her tennis shoes trampling the shine off his new boots. She was going to fall flat on her face, and take him with her!

Joshua cursed when he felt his lower lip split open. He circled his arm around her waist and staggered forward, but he couldn't quite recover his balance. Taking the brunt of the fall, he rolled backward, with Kristine's nose pressed against his chest and her fist wedged against his belly.

The next thing he knew, he was on the ground, sucking wind. Kristine was sprawled on top of him, eyes squeezed shut, panting for breath.

"Don't move," he groaned when she started to squirm. Her knee was close to an extremely vulnerable part of his anatomy. "For my sake...and the future of any unborn children I might have, don't move a muscle!"

Embarrassed by her clumsiness and by his explicitness, she growled, "Shut up."

Joshua felt as though he'd been thrown in a closet with an irate karate expert! He dabbed at his swollen lip. "You should have your elbows and feet registered with the police department as lethal weapons."

Kristie opened her eyes, assessed the bodily damage she'd caused and carefully shifted off him. Reaching into her back pocket for a handkerchief, she replied dryly, "You're going to have to concoct a wild story to explain your injuries."

"Why?"

"You're twice my size. Carlton and Drew aren't going to belive that *I* split your lip, bruised your chin and knocked you to the ground."

"Drew won't, but your dad will."

She wiped off the beginnings of his smug smile with the corner of her handkerchief. Despite the swelling, the cut was small. But a barn wasn't the most sanitary place in the world. She'd better disinfect his wound.

"Stay there. I'm going to get some antiseptic."

Her bones, having been thoroughly jarred, creaked as she rose to her feet. Almost thirty, going on eighty, she thought, hobbling to the medicine rack. But perhaps instant aging would have one advantage. Her estrogen level, which had soared out of control in the tack room, would be closer to normal.

Her eyes perused the assortment of horse medicines. She selected a plastic bottle filled with alcohol, twisted off the lid and soaked a clean section of her handkerchief with it.

"This is going to sting a little," she warned, slowly dropping to her knees.

Joshua sat up and leaned against the wall.

"Worm medicine?" he asked, looking her straight in the eye. "Guaranteed to get rid of— Ouch!"

Men are such babies, she thought, and not for the first time in her career.

"Much as I'd like to stitch your mouth shut, I don't think the injury warrants drastic medical treatment."

"Very funny, Doctor."

"About as funny as the tetanus shot I'm going to give you when we get back to the house?" A small smile tugged at the corners of her lips as she watched his eyes widen. What was it about a teeny little needle that struck terror in the heart of even the strongest man? "It won't hurt."

Unconvinced, Joshua shook his head and got to his feet. He dusted off the seat of his pants, then lightly probed his ribs where her sharp, bony elbow had to have left a purple bruise. Better to have the disease than the preventive, he thought silently.

He hated shots, and especially tetanus shots. It would make his arm sore for days. If the rough-house treatment she'd already given him was anything to go by, she'd surely administer the shot with a horse syringe!

"I'll take my chances with lockjaw," he muttered.

"A pleasant thought, but I'm afraid I have to insist on the tetanus shot." She gave him the comforting thousand-kilowatt smile she usually reserved for her patients. Unable to resist, she added, "If you don't bawl, I'll give you a great big lollipop."

The warmth of her smile almost persuaded him to follow her advice. Almost, but not quite. It wasn't as though he'd stepped on a rusty nail or scraped his hand on an old barbed-wire fence. And it wasn't as though this were the first time he'd had his lip split. He'd been one of the tallest kids in his class all throughout school, so he'd been in his share of fights.

"No thanks. I'll survive without a shot."

Kristie dogged his footsteps as he went over to Lazy Bones and walked her into her stall. She'd be guilty of gross negligence if she allowed him to talk his way out of treatment.

"And, along with your lollipop, I'll keep my mouth shut about you mauling me in the barn. You can tell Dad and Drew that you tripped and fell."

Joshua removed the bit from the horse's mouth, fervently wishing it was a muzzle that would fit Kristine's mouth. From the teasing light in those baby blues of hers, he was dead certain she was contemplating what tale she'd spin if he refused treatment.

"Or I could say you told me about taking over part of my job and we duked it out." She paused, grinned and waved her small fist at him. "I won, which means you have to get out of Dodge before sunset."

"Sounds like blackmail to me."

He gave Lazy Bones a pat, then strode from the stall to the rack where the other bridles hung. Kristie swaggered after him, sticking her thumbs in her back pockets.

"The end justifies the means," she said airily. "Like it or not, you *are* going to get a tetanus shot."

The thin fabric of her T-shirt stretched taut across her breasts, and Joshua wondered how the hell he could have mistaken her for a teenager. At the same time, he muttered a mild expletive at having noticed how well-endowed she was. His palms grew moist at the forbidden memory of his fingers cupping her derriere when she'd landed on top of him. For a scant moment his eyes moved to the soft bow of her lips.

Without answering, he tore his eyes away from her and strode down the wide corridor. She wants to give me a shot, he mused, and I'm thinking about what it would be like to kiss her? I've gone mad, completely insane!

Disgusted by his lack of control, he said, "You can tell any damn story you please. It won't be the first lie a woman's told about me."

Kristie kicked the sand with her toe, wishing it were his butt. The man had absolutely no sense of humor! That was one personality trait she'd had to develop to survive. No wonder his son hates him! Who wouldn't hate a man who couldn't laugh at himself?

Laugh, period! she told herself, modifying her diagnosis of his ailment. That mask of his would probably shatter if a chuckle passed through his lips!

She trailed slowly after him. There was no doubt in her mind that he'd be impossible to work with. Surely her father could see that. If Carlton thought she'd been harsh in her attempts to change his lackadaisically run clinics into a professional operation, he'd be most displeased with Joshua Hayden's performance.

"Good," she muttered, practicing what she planned on saying to her father. Her finger pointed at the empty space on the porch where Joshua had disappeared into the house. "You think the other doctors tried to gang up on me because I was the boss's daughter? Just wait until you see them work on giving Mr. Grim an attitude adjustment. Within a week they'll have him strapped to a table and be administering laughing gas!"

She stopped at the corral gate and cocked her head to one side as a brilliant idea formulated in her mind. As much as she liked the mental picture of Joshua Hayden gasping for breath between hoots of laughter, she liked the possibility of his being his own worst enemy more.

Why should she battle with Carlton over Joshua's hiring?

Granted, she was still miffed at him for not having consulted her before hiring Joshua, but he was her father. She'd spent a lifetime trying to get his approval. Why fight with him over Joshua when there was another viable option?

Her fingertips drummed against the weathered cedar as her alternative idea grew.

Wouldn't it be smarter to appear to go along with her father's decision and let Joshua ride roughshod over the company's employees until Carlton realized he'd made a mistake? It shouldn't take more than a month for everyone, Carlton included, to be heartily sick of him.

And the whole time he's being an ass, she mused, I'll be Miss Congeniality.

"Sweeter than honey butter," she whispered, quoting her father's description of the ideal woman.

She donned a sickly sweet smile, climbed over the gate and headed toward the house. She'd help Joshua. She could be as contradictory as he was. She'd help him all right—right out of a job.

Three

_____

What do you think of him?'' Carlton asked when they'd finished dinner.

Kristie and her father sat inside the ''bird cage,'' a screened-in pool and patio filled with tropical plants and blooming spring flowers. Since Carlton's heart attack it had become a habit for them to spend this time together on pleasant weekend evenings.

Joshua and Drew had retired to the guest suite, which, unlike the other rooms of the house, did not open onto the pool area. Their rooms adjoined a fenced patio that afforded them their own privacy.

What do I think of him? Kristie considered giving him a curt, blunt assessment of Joshua Hayden, but she refrained. All through the meal she'd had to chew on the tip of her tongue to keep from wielding it like a scalpel. She'd been charming and gracious while Joshua had mapped out the changes he planned to make. She had already presented some of the same ideas to her father—and he'd rejected them all. Her insides had been seething with contained frustration.

"He's...interesting." She gave her father a sweet smile, her face aching. He's lower than a gator's belly, she silently added.

The wary smile he gave her told her that her thoughts were transparent. Her atypical behavior toward the man who'd usurped her job had to be puzzling him.

"He's certainly well qualified," Carlton said. "Don't you think we were lucky to be able to lure him away from his job in Boston?"

Now he asks my opinion, Kristie thought, groaning, when it's too late to tear up the man's employment agreement. Didn't her father realize that Joshua had come to Florida because of Drew, not the clinics?

She held her tongue, giving a noncommittal "Mmm."

"Yes, indeed," Carlton said, leaning his head back on the plush cushion of the patio chair. "He's just what the doctor ordered—a man with an eye for details, an organizer. Do you know that while you were changing for dinner and we were in the office he asked me about the expiration date of vaccinations? He pulled a little chart out of his billfold and decided he'd better have a tetanus shot, since he would be wandering around the farm for the next few weeks. How many men do you know who have their shot records in their hip pockets?"

"None," she replied truthfully, staring into the aquamarine water of the pool as her mind coupled what her father had said with the highly libidinous thoughts she'd had while taking her shower.

Most single men his age carried other objects in their billfolds, objects that were far more revealing than a vaccination record, she thought.

"Kristine?"

"Hmm?"

"You were awfully quiet during dinner. You're being close-mouthed now. What are you thinking about so hard?"

"Men."

"Men, plural? Or man, singular, as in one man in particular—Joshua Hayden?"

Her eyes snapped from the water's depths to her father's grin. Not once in the past had he ever inquired about her feelings toward a man. There was something suspicious going on here, something very suspicious.

"Perhaps," she replied cagily.

Carlton chuckled. "It was that way between your mother and me."

"What way?"

"Instant attraction. One minute I was a carefree bachelor flirting with all the nurses and the next thing I knew—*wham*! I was in love." He cocked his head to one side. "Do you hear a peculiar ticking sound coming from the region around your heart?"

"Like a time bomb ready to go off?"

He shook his head, blithely ignoring the subtle warning tone in her voice. "Softer. More incessant. It happens when there's a child in the house of a busy career woman who's nearing thirty."

There was no mistaking exactly what he meant: her biological clock.

"Oh, yeah?" In one little move, Kristie swung her legs off her chaise lounge and stood up on the cool deck.

"Where are you going?"

"Inside—to get my stethoscope. If there's some strange ticking going on around my heart, I want to check it out. I might have inherited a genetic predisposition to heart attacks."

"That isn't what I meant," Carlton protested.

Hands on her hips, Kristie asked sweetly, "Just what did you mean?"

"Well, uh . . ." Carlton circled the back of his collar with one finger. "Joshua is unattached."

"Unattached? Where? Can we sew him back together?" she asked with feigned obtuseness.

"You know perfectly well what I mean. He's available."

"For what? Stud service for an old maid whose biological clock has its alarm bell about to ring?"

"You're taking this the wrong way, Kristine."

"Am I? Just why did you hire Joshua Hayden? Am I a hidden clause in that damn agreement you signed?"

"Of course not!"

"But wouldn't it be convenient for you if I did marry Joshua?"

"Truthfully? Yes! But I don't believe in marriages of convenience. You know I want you to marry someone you love. I want you to be happy!"

"Be happy?" Kristine groaned. Her father played this broken record every time he needed an excuse for a decision he'd made without consulting her. "Be happy! Okay, Dad. I'm happy! I'm deliriously happy that you've hired Joshua to take part of my job!"

She flashed Carlton a fake, toothy smile, then strutted around the patio, flinging her arms wide, then hugging herself.

"Look! I'm happy! Ecstatic! I'm so happy that I'm going to go to bed, right now, and dream of a handsome prince arriving on my doorstep driving a grimy Cherokee. Ah, yes, and I'll dream of the fine-looking son he brought with him to slow down the ticking noise."

"Your mother was never sarcastic," Carlton said in a voice that was barely a notch above a whisper.

She should have been able to find an answer to that mild rebuke sometime during the past twenty years, but she hadn't. One look in the mirror told her she looked like her mother, his precious, beloved wife. Why couldn't she act like her? Her face crumpled.

"I'm just me, Dad," she replied, her voice as soft as his. "I can't be her. I've tried, hard."

"I know, sweetheart."

The sadness she heard in his voice hurt even more than his calm acceptance of her inadequacies. She turned, staring at the distant, dreamy look in his eyes. Physically he was there, in the chair, gazing up at the millions of stars that lit up the sky; mentally he'd journeyed beyond space, to a place where she would be considered a trespasser.

Her heart twisted as though a cruel hand had reached inside her chest and squeezed it. She felt like sinking down on her knees beside his chair, telling him how much she loved him and begging him to love her despite her inadequacies.

Once, when she'd been six, she'd done that. He'd absently stroked her hair and told her that he loved her, too. But even at such a tender age she'd known deep in her heart that she could never take her mother's place.

He loved her mother; he only cared for her. There was a wide gap between these emotions. Hard as she tried, she'd failed to close that gap.

It was a lost cause.

"Good night, Father," she said quietly. "I love you."

"Night, love."

He'd answered distractedly, and she knew he hadn't really heard her.

She crossed through a door into the formal living room. Blinded by her inner sadness, she didn't bother to switch the lights on, so she didn't notice the man sitting in the wicker chair in the dark shadows.

For a moment, Joshua hesitated. There was something defenseless and vulnerable about her as her bare feet silently whispered across the carpet, despite the angry, sarcastic remarks he'd just heard her make about himself and Drew.

He'd listened stoically, not moving so much as a muscle. Worse had been said about him. He, too, had spoken angry words while making meaningless, empty vows to keep Drew away from his ex-wife's parents.

He understood emotional pain; the bruises didn't show, but that didn't make the wounds any less painful.

"Kristine?"

Kristie had been thinking of how her desire to please Carlton made it easy for him to manipulate her life. She jumped, then groaned. How long had Joshua been sitting there? How much had he heard? Good Lord, she hoped he hadn't been eavesdropping when she'd accused her father of hiring someone to marry her! After her unwanted physical reaction to him in the barn, he'd probably think she'd be a willing partner to any plans her father might make.

Mortified, she whirled around. "Did you get an earful?"

"I heard enough to know my being hired isn't the only problem you have."

He rose and moved slowly toward her. The woebegone expression on her face made him long to reach out to her, to give her the solace she'd sought from her father, the solace she'd been denied. Of their own accord, his hands moved toward her. The withering look she gave him resulted in their dropping back to his side.

"What do you want, Joshua? You've already stripped me of part of my job. What's next? My pride? Does it thrill you to discover there's a rift between Carlton and myself?"

"No. No more than I'm thrilled with the breach between Drew and myself." His fingers itched to wipe away the diamondlike tears gathered on the tips of her lashes. He shoved his hands into his pockets. "I came looking for you because..." He lowered his voice, reluctant to ask a favor of her. "I need your help."

"Are you out of your ever-lovin' mind?"

"It appears so," he admitted ruefully. "While Drew was getting ready for bed he was babbling on and on about what an awesome lady you are."

Kristie had the grace to blush; remembering her thoughts about Joshua's son during dinner had not been nearly so kind. She liked Drew, but she didn't want his dark, puppylike eyes worshipping her the way they had at dinner. And she sure as hell didn't want Drew to develop a crush on her!

"And," Joshua continued, squelching a pang of jealousy, the same jealousy he'd felt as he'd listened to Drew, "while we may not be fans of each other, we might combine forces to keep my son from pestering you."

"I'm capable of saying no." She'd learned how to do that during her residency; several of the male residents had erroneously believed that a medical degree made a man God's gift to women. Surely she could dampen Drew's puppy love. "He won't be a pest."

"Okay. Then let's say I want to make up for the disappointment caused by your putting him on a horse and me ordering him down."

Her gaze slid guiltily to her toes. She had unintentionally caused additional friction between Joshua and his son. But, she told herself, everything would have been fine and dandy if Joshua had stayed in the house until Drew had ridden around the corral a couple of times.

"So? You take him horseback riding tomorrow."

"That's what I suggested to Drew. In two seconds flat he pointed out that I can run a hospital single-handed, but I haven't been on a horse since I was a teenager. According to him, that was several centuries ago. I promised him I'd convince you to go with us." He knew he was taking unfair advantage of her soft heart when he added, "He hugged me. It's the first time he's touched me spontaneously since he was five years old."

Standing less than a foot from him, Kristie fought the magnetic pull of his strong will. She ached to accede to his request, but she forced herself to say, "You do have a problem."

Their eyes met; blue clashed with brown. She'd have been able to stick to her decision to refuse his invitation if he hadn't touched her. His palm curved around her jaw, his smallest finger resting on the erratic pulse beating in her throat.

"Please," he whispered, drawing closer and bending his head toward her. "Don't make me disappoint Drew again."

"You shouldn't make promises you can't keep."

Her eyes focused on the tiny disfigurement on his lower lip. As a good doctor she'd disinfected the cut with antiseptic. But as a woman she had to fight the desire to kiss it and make it better.

Her throat went dry, and she swallowed, hard. His thumb stroked her neck as though to soothe it.

"Will you go with us?"

She wanted to block the urgency she heard in his voice from reaching her ears, her heart. The fragrance of his woodsy after-shave teased her nose until she longed to edge closer to him. His body heat radiated around her.

And her father picked that moment to turn on the stereo and play his favorite Jackie Gleason album, *For Lovers Only*. The sexy music wafted in through the open patio doors.

With her last ounce of willpower, she clamped her lips shut to keep back the unwanted reply: *Anywhere.*

His thumb moved across her Cupid's-bow lips until they refused to heed the command from her brain and parted. It was all she could do to keep the tip of her tongue from flicking across his thumb to taste his salty flesh.

Her eyes raised back up to his, no longer defiant. "What time?"

Kristie wasn't the only one fighting the power of soft music, tantalizing fragrances and unwanted physical need. Joshua's fingertips felt as though they'd caught on fire when her hot breath caressed them.

Primitive urges had his heart pounding in his chest. He wanted to pick her up and carry her to the nearest bed, as one of his caveman ancestors might have done.

"Early. Eight?"

"Before breakfast?"

His dark eyes tasted her lips as though their strawberry coloring held the exotic flavors of paradise.

"Yes."

She nodded; her lips brushed the palm of his hand. It wasn't a kiss, she told herself, but the hint of a smile on his lips told her otherwise.

A rosy pinkness suffused her cheeks. What must he be thinking? First she'd knocked him down and wallowed on the floor with him, and now she was kissing his hand!

Calling on her last reserves of strength, she stepped back, appalled by the tripping of her heart. He smiled widely and she cataloged her symptoms: flushed face, irregular heartbeat, sweaty palms, a sappy grin on her own face!

Happiness? She retreated another three steps. Seeing Joshua Hayden smile made her happy? Heavens above, she had to get some distance between them so that she could analyze the data. Her diagnosis had to be wrong.

Her retreat aroused another unfamiliar and primitive instinct in Joshua—the instinct to stalk the prey until it was in one's clutches. Only the thin civilized veneer bred into him over hundreds of generations allowed him to remain motionless.

"G'night, Kristine. Sweet dreams."

Hours later, Kristie was pacing the floor in her bedroom, wondering if his polite words had actually been a curse! Only Sigmund Freud would have classified her dreams as sweet!

She cast a scratchy-eyed glance at her bed. The top sheet was twisted into a knot; her pillow had dents where her fist had pounded out their frustration.

Although she'd counseled other women on everything from insomnia to the normal sexual drives every woman has, she'd never fallen victim to the combined impact of the two. She'd followed her own prescription for torrid dreams. Thirst—the body crying out for water—often caused them.

She'd gulped down three glasses of tepid water.

And gone to the bathroom—another of nature's calls.

She'd put on a relaxation tape and listened to waves crashing on a beach, flutes playing softly in the background.

That helped loads, Kristie thought wryly. It conjured up a new setting for a love scene in glorious Technicolor between herself and Joshua! Moonlit sky, pounding surf, sand beneath her backside. Yes, indeed, it was a big help!

Ever since Joshua and Drew Hayden had arrived, her world had been upside down, inside out, topsy-turvy.

"And I don't like it," she said aloud, in the hope of convincing herself. "I don't want complications in my life. I sure as hell don't want a man in there mucking up my plans!"

She wanted desperately to hate Joshua.

Pacing back and forth, she'd recited all the valid reasons she had to hate him. He'd been hired, without her father's consulting her, to take away part of her job. He would cause the gap between her and Carlton to widen once they no longer had the business end of the clinics as a mutual bond.

For heaven's sake, his own kid disliked him. That alone was enough to warrant detesting the man! Children had a natural talent for separating the good guys from the bad guys. Who better than Joshua's own flesh and blood to know what a miserable, cruel person he had to be?

So how'd he get such gentle hands?

What makes you feel as though you could drown in those soulful black eyes of his?

What is there about him that makes you want to grab him and hold on tight?

Damned if she knew!

The way he made her feel had nothing to do with logic or rational behavior. Maybe he wasn't really from Boston. Maybe he hailed from Salem. His being a warlock was the only sane explanation for the spell he seemed to have cast over her.

"That's ridiculous," she muttered.

The only rational explanation for the effect he had on her was a hormone imbalance; her estrogen level must be out of synch.

She crossed to the bathroom once again and eyed the tiny pills in the disc-shaped container in the medicine cabinet. The birth control pills she took daily to regulate her monthly cycle must be causing the problem. Her stomach had been somewhat queasy. Her fingers skimmed over her satin nightgown. Her breasts did feel enlarged, tender. She hadn't experienced leg cramps, but she had felt weak in the knees.

Satisfied that she'd finally found a logical scientific explanation for her peculiar symptoms, she went back to her bed, straightened the sheets and slid between them.

There had to be a simple scientific reason for her insomnia, too. She toyed with the idea of writing a prescription for sleeping pills but discarded it. Smart doctors don't self-medicate. It was the easiest, most dangerous trap a medical professional could fall into.

"One sleepless night isn't insomnia," she mumbled, and felt a rush of adrenaline pump through her system when she closed her eyes and saw a pair of dark eyes smiling at her. She prescribed the safest medicine known to the medical profession: letting nature take its course.

It did.

By the next morning, Kristie's sweet dreams had faded back into her subconscious. Surprisingly, she felt terrific. Eager to saddle up her favorite Arabian mare, Misty Blue, and follow the winding trail that led to the private lake at the back of the Fairbanks property, she rolled out of bed and dashed to the bathroom.

A splash of cold water on her face washed away the hazy residue of her dreams and brought reality back into focus. She wouldn't be riding alone today, as she normally did on Sunday mornings. She'd agreed to let Joshua and Drew accompany her.

Patting her face dry with a fluffy towel, she began to consider which horses she'd have them ride. Lazy Bones was perfect for an completely inexperienced rider like Drew. But which horse, she wondered, suited Joshua?

A wicked gleam shone from her blue eyes as she lowered the towel and glanced in the mirror.

"Whiskey?"

The chestnut-colored quarter horse looked like a dilapidated bag of bones, but he had a mean streak that ran from his inch-long teeth to his sharp hooves. His reputation for biting, bucking and kicking contrasted sharply with his swaybacked appearance.

Grinning, she whispered to her reflection, "You wouldn't do that to Joshua, would you?"

Her head bobbed up and down.

"Nah, you can't do that to him! Whiskey would toss Joshua off his back and spoil the crease in those pressed jeans of his. You wouldn't make him eat dirt just because you lost a little sleep over him, would you? Never mind the fact that he's taking over the financial reins of the Fairbanks Care Centers."

Her head bobbed up and down again.

"After he picks himself up off the ground, he'll be furious. But you don't care, do you?"

Her head should have waggled from side to side; it remained motionless.

You do care!

She shook her head in a vehement denial.

"Whiskey and Joshua Hayden are a perfect match. Contradictory. Stubborn. Hardmouthed."

She flung the towel over the rack and took another hard look at herself in the mirror. Close scrutiny revealed that fatigue had etched faint lines around her eyes. The purple smudges beneath her eyes testified to a night spent tossing and turning and twisting the sheets into knots.

"Whiskey it is," she told herself. "Woe be unto Joshua Hayden!"

"Whoa!" Dusty ordered, grinning like the Cheshire cat at Kristie.

She'd told him who Joshua was and why he was at the ranch, and he'd gleefully gone about following her instructions. He wouldn't have made it easy for any man who was trying to replace him. It wasn't that Dusty was a vindictive man, but he readily admitted to being possessive about his job and about Kristie Fairbanks.

Dusty had already saddled up Lazy Bones and Misty Blue and watched as Drew had climbed aboard his horse like an old ranch hand. Now Joshua had one hand on Lazy Bones's reins and both eyes on Kristie's tight jeans. Dusty didn't like that one little bit. To his way of thinking, Joshua Hayden needed to keep his fingers out of Kristie's pie and his damn eyes off her derriere!

"Here you go, *Mr.* Hayden," he said, shoving Whiskey's reins into Joshua's hand to distract him. "You and Whiskey ought to get along just fine."

Joshua watched as Whiskey rolled his eyes and flared his nostrils. A sharp glance at the horse's bloated sides made him wary. The saddle's cinch appeared tight, but he felt certain that once the horse heaved the air out of his lungs the saddle would slip and he'd be riding Whiskey's belly.

Joshua might have new clothes, but Dusty and Kristie had jumped to the wrong conclusion. Yes, he'd been born and raised in a metropolitan area, but he'd spent two summers on his great-uncle's ranch in Wyoming. He knew a mean horse when he saw one.

Joshua took the reins, cursing himself for having trusted a woman. He should have known the lyrical tone of her voice and the submissive looks she'd been giving him for what they were—the signs of a woman's wiles.

His gut twisted into a knot tighter than the horse's cinch belt. He knew better than to trust a woman. Hadn't his ex-wife lured him into bed with her feminine wiles, then kicked his ass out when he'd served his purpose?

Fool, he silently told himself. Only a fool fell into the same trap twice. He hadn't meant to embarrass Kristine last night by mentioning that he'd overheard Carlton's remarks about marriage, and her response, but he had. Letting him make an ass out of himself in front of Drew must be Kristine's way of taking her revenge.

Well, the little lady is in for a surprise, he mused. Thanks to his previous experience, he could handle Whiskey—and her—with one hand tied behind his back. He wouldn't fall off the damn horse, and he wouldn't fall for Kristine's tricks.

"Wait a minute!" Kristie called. "Whiskey's up to his old tricks."

She brushed past Dusty, unbuckled the cinch circling Whiskey's bloated middle and kneaded the horse until air whistled through his nostrils. Dusty had taken her instructions too literally. She'd wanted to bruise Joshua's male pride, not break every bone in his body!

"C'mon, Dad!" Drew said impatiently. "Hop in the saddle and let's get goin'."

Kristie hesitated, keeping Joshua from obeying his son's command. She caught her lower lip between her teeth in consternation as her conscience prodded her hard.

It was one thing to cheerfully watch Joshua eat dust; it was another for him to be seen eating dirt by Drew. She wouldn't be able to live with herself if she harmed a man's relationship with his son.

"I'll ride Whiskey," she said, swiftly grabbing the reins and springing into the saddle. "You ride Misty Blue."

Predictablly, Whiskey remained stationary. He wouldn't act up until the corral gate was open and he could get the bit between his teeth. Then all hell would break loose.

From the corner of his eye Joshua watched Dusty's jaw drop to his chest. Suspicions confirmed, he mused, wondering what had caused Kristine to change her mind. He eyed her slender wrists and hands. One hard toss of Whiskey's head and the horse could put her right out of business. A doctor couldn't heal the sick and wounded with both wrists in casts.

"Misty Blue is your regular mount, isn't she?"

His eyes moved to the beautiful little mare. He figured Kristie had altered her plan. She wouldn't attempt to break his neck; she'd only have to take care of him if she did. She'd just make him look foolish in front of his son. While she was impressing Drew with an exhibition of horsemanship, he'd be looking ridiculous, with his long legs dangling down Misty Blue's sides and his feet nearly scraping the ground.

"Yeah, but she's well trained. You won't have any problems." I'll be the one with my hands full of problems, she added silently.

She settled deeper in the saddle, preparing to hang on for dear life. The stirrups had been adjusted to suit Joshua's long legs. She started to readjust them.

She wanted to lean forward and whisper soothingly to Whiskey that going beyond the corral gate didn't mean he was being ridden straight to the glue factory, but if she did Joshua would overhear her. She pasted a sickly-sweet smile on her face.

"She's too short in the poop for a man my size," Joshua drawled, imitating his great uncle's slow Western drawl. "Get off Whiskey. I'll ride him."

Kristie's mind raced. What should she do now?

"You heard the man, Kristie," Dusty said, afraid his trick was going to backfire in his face. "He *wants* to ride Whiskey."

"C'mon, Dad! Get on a horse! Any horse! Are we gonna sit around here arguing all day?"

Dusty grabbed at Whiskey's reins and Kristie heard the horse's teeth snap on the stainless-steel bit. He moved to the opposite side of the horse from Joshua and whispered, "Have you lost your mind? Do what the man says!"

"No!"

"Yes," Joshua said, snaking his arm around Kristine's waist and pulling her from the saddle. When she squirmed in his arms, he said, in a voice that was half groan, half growl, "You're going to have to get used to taking orders from me, Doctor."

That was enough to put the starch back in her shirt collar.

"The minute you mount that horse you're going to find out who's the boss around here," she told him, gritting her teeth.

She batted at the hands that were holding her close to his chest, inadvertently burying her nose in the crisp hairs above the buttons of his shirt. Her heart skipped a beat when he planted her feet firmly on the ground.

"I can take care of myself."

"You heard the man," Dusty said, relieved to see the original plan back in action. Carlton would be advertising for a new horse trainer if Kristie insisted on being a heroine and broke her fool neck.

"Dad!"

Joshua vaulted into the saddle, hoping no one would notice the traitorous response of the hard flesh that had been pressing against her. There was more than one way for her to embarrass him in front of his son. He wasn't about to let any of them happen!

Before Kristie could warn him about exactly what he could expect from Whiskey once they were outside the gate, Joshua and Drew were across the corral and Dusty was chuckling as he opened the gate.

Kristie watched aghast as Whiskey walked through the opening, as docile as if he'd been given a bucketful of tranquilizers with his morning feed.

"Well, I'll be a damn bob-tail polecat," Dusty muttered under his breath, scratching at the gray stubble on his chin.

"Whazzat mean, Dad?"

Joshua reined in Whiskey. He grinned over his shoulder at Drew. "He's describing a skunk, son. We'll have to keep an eye out for the other little stinker, won't we?"

Drew hooted. "You mean Kristine?"

At that instant, Whiskey decided to play one of his old tricks. His hind legs shot out from under him, then thudded back to the ground. Joshua's teeth rattled.

Joshua shortened the reins to prevent Whiskey from getting the bit between his teeth. "Stay with Kristine," he told Drew. "I'll have to ride the meanness right out of this one." He gave Whiskey a flick with his heels, and the ornery gelding galloped down the trail toward the lake.

Mounted, Kristie walked Misty Blue through the gate, watching Joshua handle Whiskey like an Olympic equestrian. She gave a slight shrug of her shoulders when Dusty shot her a puzzled look. What could she say? She'd misjudged Joshua.

"Wow!" Drew said, his voice filled with pride. "Lookit my dad ride. Awesome, huh?"

"Awesome," Kristie repeated, though with something less than enthusiasm. Aware that Drew wanted to gallop after his father, she added, "We'll take it slow and easy."

"Aw, Kristine... This is easy. Don't you start treating me like a baby."

She heard his protest, but she also saw his Adam's apple bob when he looked down at the ground and saw his hand drop to the saddle horn.

"You'll be riding like your dad in no time," she promised him, smiling at his bravado. She made a clicking noise and skirted Misty Blue in front of Lazy Bones. Saving Drew's pride by blocking the path of his mount, she called over her shoulder, "The trail narrows up ahead."

Ten minutes down the trail, Kristie began to worry. Joshua had vanished like a puff of trail dust. She braced her feet in the stirrups and raised herself up in the saddle, scanning the flat, open pasture. Black oaks dripping with Spanish moss lined the edge of the field and hampered her view.

"Do you see your dad?"

"He's probably already at the lake. He's going lickety-split and we're going at a snail's pace. We'll never catch up."

"It's a quarter of a mile from here to the fence. Want to trot up to the gate?"

Drew nudged Lazy Bones's sides. The mare snorted but kept plodding along.

"He won't go!"

Kristie grinned, her eyes filled with amusement. "Maybe you ought to practice some good manners—in horse language."

"Good manners in horse language?" Drew echoed skeptically.

"You're supposed to say 'please' when you want something and 'thank you' when you've got enough, right?"

"Yeah."

"In horse language, 'giddyap' means 'please go' and 'whoa' means stop."

"Giddyap, Lazy Bones!"

Much to Drew's delight, Lazy Bones pricked up her ears and picked up her hooves. Butt bouncing up and down in the saddle, elbows flapping, Drew squealed with pleasure.

"Hey! Faster, Lazy Bones! Giddyap!"

"Don't go past the gate," Kristie called, letting him jostle along. Later Joshua could show him how to sit a trotting horse without looking like a flustered chicken. That's if Whiskey hasn't transported Joshua across the state line! she added mentally.

Four

—

You cantankerous cross between a swamp rabbit and a Missouri mule! Have you had enough?"

Joshua wondered if the Fairbankses realized they had one hell of a jumper. Whiskey had cleared two fences, a creek and God only knew how much scrub brush. Joshua had been too busy trying to stay in the saddle to keep track.

The closer they'd come to Juniper Lake, the more certain Joshua had been that the damn horse wanted to jump that, too.

The ten-foot-long alligators basking in the warm rays of the morning sun had deterred Whiskey from attempting that feat.

"You should have been named Mercury."

He swung down from the saddle and suddenly had second thoughts about renaming the horse. Staggering, barely able to keep his balance, he realized that the horse had the same effect on him as a bottle of Kentucky's best whiskey.

"There he is!" Drew shouted over his shoulder to Kristie. "Hey, Dad! Look at me ride! Giddyap, Lazy Bones!"

Kristie looped the wire that closed the gate over the two fenceposts. "Don't get too near the water!"

Lazy Bones charged toward the lake at a full gallop.

Joshua waved his arms, crisscrossing them over his head, to signal to Drew to stop before he plunged into the alligator-infested lake. He heard his son's voice crack when he sighted the reptiles and shouted, "Whoa! Please! I mean, giddyap!"

His short legs squeezed the horse's middle tighter and tighter, urging the horse forward. He tried to kick his feet out of the stirrups and his heels repeatedly jabbed Lazy Bones in the sides.

"No, Drew! Stop gigging her!" Kristie screamed. She flattened herself across Misty Blue's neck, urging her mount to go faster and faster. Her smaller horse rapidly closed the gap, but Kristie knew she'd never make it in time to cut in front of Lazy Bones.

"Stop, horse! Stop!" Drew cried, dropping the reins and hanging on to the saddle horn. "Stop!"

Joshua straddled Whiskey and raced toward the lake, his heart pounding. He thought he'd make it until he saw a monstrous alligator slithering up the path, directly in front of Lazy Bones.

As he drew alongside Lazy Bones, Joshua could hear the alligator hiss an ominous warning. He hooked his arms around Drew's waist and jerked his reins to the right. Lazy Bones reared, then veered to the left. Drew clung to Joshua's neck, shaking, crying, muttering to himself.

Kristie reined in Misty Blue in time to see Joshua hugging his son close, saying, "You're safe, son. I've got you." Drew was crying, but returning his father's embrace.

Realizing that father and son needed privacy, Kristie turned Misty Blue toward the stand of oak trees where Lazy Bones had stopped to graze.

"Thank God Joshua can ride like the wind," she murmured to Misty Blue. "We'd never have made it in time."

She wiped the perspiration from her brow with her sleeve. Drew might have been mauled by the alligator. She blamed herself for not having warned him of the dangers surrounding most Florida lakes. But she'd had no idea he'd take off like a bullet fired from a six-shooter the moment he saw his father.

Joshua wiped away the tears of relief streaming down Drew's face with his handkerchief. He hadn't quite realized just how young his son was until he'd held him in his arms and listened to him sob out his fear. Because Drew had been so damn belligerent and defiant, Joshua had been treating him like a miniature adult.

"I couldn't stop Lazy Bones," Drew blubbered. "I said 'please' and 'thank you' in horse talk. The reins fell out of my hand. My foot got stuck and that—that alligator wanted to eat me!"

Joshua gave his son's cheeks a final swipe. "Blow."

"You're never gonna let me ride again, are you?"

"Not alone," Joshua said. "Not for a while, anyway."

"I just wanted to ride into the water like they do in the movies," the boy said, pinching his nose with the handkerchief and blowing hard. "I didn't know there would be dinosaurs on the bank."

"Dinosaurs?"

"They may look like alligators to you, but from where I was sitting the one with its mouth open looked like a dinosaur. Its jaws had to be at least a mile wide." He wiped his nose, sniffed, then returned his father's grin. "I thought Lazy Bones and me would fit right inside those jaws and it would swallow us whole!"

"I wouldn't have let that happen to you." Joshua gave his son a manly hug, glad he could joke about the near-tragedy. "I'd have thought of something to get you out of the dinosaur's stomach."

"Red pepper." Drew shoved the hankie in his back pocket and jumped to the ground. "Makes 'em sneeze. I saw it on TV."

"I think we'd better make a few trips to the local library, son. Get you away from the boob tube."

"Kristine's coming." Drew held out his hand as his father dismounted also. "You won't tell her I bawled, will you? I don't want her to think I'm a baby."

Joshua took his son's offered hand; his knees were shaking again. He'd be sore tomorrow, damn sore.

"Don't be ashamed of crying, Drew. Grown men cry when they're scared or hurt, too."

"Yeah?"

"Yeah."

He tousled Drew's dark hair and watched as he raced toward his horse, remembering the tears he'd cried the day he'd lost custody of his son. And the tears of joy he'd cried, in the privacy of a stall in the men's washroom, the day he'd been awarded custody.

Joshua understood how his son felt. At his age, hadn't his own father told him to swallow his tears? Grown men weren't supposed to cry. He wouldn't teach his son that archaic lesson. He'd learned the hard way.

In moments of deep anguish or great joy, a man shouldn't be ashamed of showing his emotions.

"I almost had Lazy Bones stopped," Drew told Kristie. "But I was real glad when Dad jerked me off her back."

"I should have warned you, but I wanted to see the look on your face the first time you saw them. Sorry, Drew."

Kristie glanced anxiously at Joshua. Did he blame her? If she hadn't chosen Whiskey as his mount he'd have been right beside his son. Was he ready to sink his teeth into her—as ready as the alligator had been to sink its teeth into Drew—for putting his son in danger?

"It wasn't your fault," Drew told her. "I'm awful thirsty, though. Do you think we could go back to the house for something to drink?"

"That sounds good to me," Joshua said, dreading the thought of another wild bronco ride back to the barn.

He was one long ache, from the small of his back to his knees. Leading Whiskey by the reins, he strode toward them.

"Need a boost up?" Kristie asked, grinning, as Drew tried to get his foot into the stirrups.

Joshua handed Kristie Whiskey's reins. "I'll help him." He laced his fingers together. "Put your foot in here."

Drew winced when his backside hit the saddle. "My butt's a little sore."

"So's mine," Joshua admitted. He held one hand out for the reins and rubbed his tender backside with the other. "So's mine!"

"Does that mean nobody wants to race back to the house?" Kristie asked shamelessly.

Father and son groaned in unison.

This time, however, Whiskey was content to amble along beside Lazy Bones.

"Guess you showed him who's boss, huh, Dad?"

"Purely a temporary truce." He glanced at Drew and Kristine, wondering if the same could be said about them. He hoped he could have a permanent truce with them both. He didn't think his poor old bones were up to a rematch—with woman, child or horse!

"I've got some liniment back at the barn that'll take care of those sore muscles," Kristie said. "It stinks to high heaven, but it works wonders."

"More horse medicine?" Joshua asked. The tip of his tongue skated across his lower lip. "Are you certain you aren't a horse doctor in disguise?"

Kristie shook her head. At one time she'd wanted to get her degree in veterinarian medicine, but a medical degree had meant that she could help Carlton. Her first priority had been pleasing him. Maybe she'd made the wrong choice. A business degree or a hospital administration degree would have been more useful to him. But as soon as the thought came to her she dismissed it.

The thought of spending her entire day shuffling papers made her cringe. Her reasons for going into medicine might have been misguided, but she loved her work.

"Where'd you learn to ride, Dad?"

For the remainder of the ride back to the barn, Kristie listened to Drew quizzing his father as if he were a stranger he wanted to get to know. Joshua gave him a couple of friendly pointers on how to allow the rhythm of the horse to keep his bottom from bouncing in the saddle. Drew followed his father's example and tucked his elbows close to his ribs.

Yesterday she'd have sworn a civil exchange between them was impossible. Funny, she mused, how shared danger had broken through Drew's hostility.

Dusty climbed down from the cedar fence where he'd been waiting for them and opened the corral gate.

"Now I know why cowboys are bowlegged," Drew said to Dusty. He made a comical face as he dismounted. "I sure could use a sasparilla. Where's the nearest saloon?"

"Maude has pancakes and maple syrup waiting for you in the kitchen." He grabbed the back of Drew's shirt when the boy dropped Lazy Bones's reins and turned toward the house. "A cowboy always tends to his horse before he looks after himself. You lead Lazy Bones into the barn and I'll be right in to help you unsaddle her and pick her hooves."

Joshua felt older than Methuselah as he hooked his right leg over the saddle horn and slid to the ground. He hobbled around Whiskey to help Kristine off her horse.

She obviously doesn't need my help, he mused, watching her dismount gracefully.

Dusty impaled him with a take-care-of-your-own-horse look, took Misty Blue's reins and handed Kristie an envelope. "Carlton left this for you."

"Oh?" She slit the back flap of the envelope with her fingernail. "Where is he?"

Dusty glanced at his watch. Carlton had hightailed it out of there over an hour ago with one of his fishing cronies. "He should be at the Orlando airport by now."

Kristie quickly scanned her father's note. "He's gone fishing in the Bahamas?"

"Any directives for me?" Joshua asked.

"I'm supposed to show you around the clinics and be helpful. He says he's left some papers on his desk that he wants taken care of immediately." She folded the note slowly and returned it to the envelope. "Carlton mentioned something about wanting to take a fishing trip with a couple of his friends, but it's out of character for him to fly off on such short notice. Did he say anything to you, Dusty?"

"Nope. Just that he was goin' to be gone for a short spell and for me to take care of lookin' after the ranch. Maude's supposed to look after the kid while you two were workin'." He glanced at Joshua. "I reckon Doc's skedaddling out of here like a scalded cat has something to do with hiring you to run the clinics. He's gonna find out if you're worth your salt real quick-like."

Joshua nodded. He wasn't afraid to take up the challenge. "The hospital's nurses were painting picket signs when I started my last job. I can manage."

Kristie knew better than to think that Carlton just had his eye on Joshua. He wasn't the only one being tested. She'd watched how Carlton handled personnel problems. When two doctors in the same clinic were squabbling over professional duties he stepped back and adopted a let-'em-sink-or-swim attitude. The problems were solved to the satisfaction of both doctors or Carlton started interviewing for replacements. She'd have given odds that Carlton had planned this trip the day he'd hired Joshua.

He never played favorites.

She could work as a team member or look for another job, partnership or no partnership. Sink or swim. Faced with those alternatives, she knew what had to be done.

Addressing Joshua, she said, "After we've taken care of the horses and had breakfast we'd better go into

Dad's office and start dividing up who's going to do what for the next couple of weeks.''

"Me and the boy can take care of the horses," Dusty offered. "It'll keep Drew busy and out of your hair."

"Thanks, Dusty."

Not waiting for Joshua to agree or disagree with her suggestion, Kristie marched toward the house. She was none too pleased about her father's abrupt departure. The least he could have done was tell her how to reach him in case of an emergency.

Joshua handed Whiskey's reins to Dusty, but his dark eyes followed Kristine. "I appreciate your keeping an eye on Drew."

"You just keep your eyes off Kristie, and you and the boy will both stay out of trouble." Dusty muttered the warning under his breath. It was meant for Joshua's ears alone. "Part of my job is to take care of Kristie when Carlton isn't around, so I'll be keepin' an eagle eye on you, too."

Joshua frowned. He'd been completely unaware that he was following her with his eyes. He felt like an overweight sleepwalker who'd been caught raiding the refrigerator. "I'll watch myself."

He went straight to the kitchen. He stopped outside the door, his hand on the knob, looking in at Kristie's profile. She sat at the dinette table staring at the stack of pancakes Maude had served her. Tendrils of sun-kissed hair had fallen from the combs that had swept them to the crown of her head. Her pert nose flared as the aroma of maple syrup teased her appetite, but her hands remained folded in her lap.

"You clean your plate, young lady. I know your daddy leaving without so much as saying goodbye has upset you, but moping around here won't bring him home one day sooner.''

Kristie picked up the fork beside her plate and cut into the fluffy pancakes. For Maude's sake, she forked a small bite into her mouth. She could have been chewing sawdust and not have noticed.

"We'll have to manage without him," she said softly.

"You and Joshua will do fine."

Remembering Joshua's gentle touch when he'd asked her to ride with them this morning, and how he'd broken through Drew's defenses with his kindness, Kristie had to agree with Maude. Contrary to her first impression, Joshua Hayden was one of the most sensitive men she'd ever met. Along with the compelling physical attraction she felt toward him, she'd found herself genuinely liking him.

Twice this morning he'd had every right to let his temper explode—when she'd chosen Whiskey for him to ride and then when Drew had galloped into a dangerous situation. If she'd been in his shoes she'd have hurled a string of expletives at him.

She took another bite, wondering if Drew's change of attitude had contributed to Joshua's tolerance. Or maybe, in spite of her dirty trick, Joshua was beginning to like her, too. That thought appealed to her. Slowly she chewed her food, gradually becoming aware of the delicious taste.

"Is that you out there, Joshua?" Maude bustled across the kitchen, wiping her hands on her apron. "What are you doing standing there with your nose pressed up against the windowpane? Come on in here. You can keep Kristie company while I fix your pancakes."

The door creaked when Joshua opened it. Good thing it was Dusty's wife and not Dusty himself fussing at him for watching Kristine, he mused as he entered the kitchen. He'd been warned. Never mind his being twice Dusty's size and half his age; Joshua had the feeling that Kristine's sidekick would protect her to his dying breath.

"Hungry?" Kristie asked.

"A little," he admitted. His eyes slipped from the blueness of her eyes to her mouth as the tip of her tongue darted out to catch a droplet of syrup. His heart skipped a beat. "Usually I only have coffee and toast."

Maude plunked a towering plate of pancakes in front of him. "You could use a little fattening up. Anyone who can't pinch an inch doesn't have—" She bit off the last word, fanned at the pink tinge flooding her cheeks and bustled back to the stove.

Kristine grinned. She knew Maude's outlandish opinions about skinny people. Curiosity was stamped all over Joshua's face. Her eyes sparkled with mischief as she leaned toward him and mouthed, "Love handles."

"Don't you be whispering secrets, Kristie Fairbanks. You mind your manners."

The rumbling of the suppressed chuckles coming from Joshua sparked Kristie's eyes with laughter. "Yes, ma'am."

"And save your sassy mouth for Dusty."

"Yes, ma'am."

Maude muttered dire threats about what happened to little girls who grew too big for their britches while Joshua and Kristie devoured their pancakes. Between bites, Kristie caught him smiling and nodding his head at Maude's comment about her.

"Can we be excused?" Kristie asked dutifully when they'd both finished.

"I reckon."

Kristie picked up both plates and carried them to the sink. She tried to get a peek at Maude's face, but the older woman thwarted her by turning toward the stove. She was fairly sure Maude and Joshua were both grinning. "Do you want me to load the dishwasher?"

"Nope. The boy hasn't had breakfast."

"Are you mad?"

"I ought to be—you blabbing my secrets." Maude's gray eyes were as bright as newly minted silver dollars when she playfully swatted Kristie on the backside. "Both of you just get on out of here, woman. I've got work to do."

"Thanks for breakfast," Joshua said. When Kristine passed him, he looped one arm over her shoulder and fell into step beside her. "Did Maude really make you pick your own switch to be spanked with when you were little?"

"Yeah. You should have seen me in the backyard, testing them to see which one would hurt the least. But Maude must have watched, because she didn't use the fragile twig I brought back to the kitchen."

"Smart woman," Joshua remarked. His hand trailed over Kristie's bare arm. He enjoyed the feel of her as much as he did the melodic sound of her voice.

"I thought I was," she said, deliberately misconstruing his meaning.

"I meant Maude. You weren't a smart *woman* when she had you picking switches."

Kristie grinned and batted her eyelashes at him. "Last week I was. What do you think all those sticks are doing lined up in the backyard?"

"You're kidding me." He stopped and turned her to face him. "You are, aren't you?"

Actually, with his hand wreaking gentle havoc on her heart and her eyelashes fanning the air, she'd have called it flirting. Her head tilted back. She loved seeing those smiles of his that caused tiny lines to radiate from the corners of his eyes, but her gaze only reached his mouth.

"Kristine?"

The sound of her name on his lips sent crazy tingles racing down her spine. She wondered what would happen if she circled his neck with her arms, raised herself up on tiptoe and kissed him. Her lips parted. She wanted to kiss him, but she lacked the gumption to take the initiative.

Joshua's fingers tightened on her arms. He recognized her kiss-me look. He wanted to kiss her. It would be so easy to lower his mouth to hers, but, Lord have mercy, it would complicate things. His Adam's apple bobbed as he fought to contain the desire seeping through the pores of his skin.

"Yes," Kristie said, not in reply to his question, but in reply to the message she read in his intensely dark eyes.

Expending his last ounce of willpower, he stepped away from her. "Business." He gulped. "Carlton left papers on his desk."

Disappointment screamed along Kristie's nerves. Why hadn't he kissed her? He must have known she wanted him to kiss her!

Pride gave her the strength to turn away from him and move toward the office. Her feet felt as though they weighed a ton, but if he wanted to take care of business, by damn, that was what they'd do.

Joshua plowed his fingers through his hair. Damn! He'd handled that badly. Silently he called himself a thousand kinds of fool for mishandling her, but he knew a friendly kiss wouldn't have been enough to satisfy the craving he felt for her.

Frustrated, he shoved his hands in his pockets. He wanted Kristine. In another time, in another place, under different circumstances, he would have pursued her. But not here, not now. Not with the animosity she felt toward him over the clinic, and not with his unsolved problems with Drew.

His feet dragged as he moved to the doorway of Carlton's office. He couldn't stop himself from looking at her. She was curled up in the leather desk chair, her bare feet neatly tucked under her, already hunched over a pile of paperwork. She'd tucked her sun-streaked blond hair behind her ears, all except for the long strand that she was worrying with her fingers. Twin vertical lines marred the smoothness of her brow as she flipped one sheet over, then another. He could tell she was searching for something that she hadn't found yet.

Aware that he was staring at her—again—he endeavored to figure out what there was about her that drew and held his attention. Why did watching her fidgeting with her hair make him want to remove it from her fingers to see if it felt as silky as it looked? Why did he want to smooth away her worry lines with butterfly kisses?

It wasn't as if she were extremely beautiful or outrageously sexy. And it wasn't as if she were some clinging vine of a woman who begged prettily for a man to stop in and take the weight of responsibility off her shoulders. Those were his ex-wife's traits.

Kristine Fairbanks had made it perfectly clear that those small hands of hers could handle any job.

Was it her self-assuredness? No, he'd worked with a legion of competent women. He'd respected them, appreciated their insights and their contributions, but he hadn't been drawn to them.

Why couldn't he put his finger on what there was about her that attracted him?

Kristie caught a glimpse of his long shadow on the Persian carpet. She swiveled around and motioned for him to come into the office. Rejection had made her irritable. If he was going to get the credit for the business running smoothly, he might as well get the headaches, too.

"Letters of complaint," she said succinctly.

The muscles in his backside knotted in protest as he pulled a chair up beside the desk and sat down gingerly. Air whistled through his teeth when his buttocks made contact with the chair.

Kristie noticed his discomfort. "Ten minutes in a hot Jacuzzi would help those sore muscles. Followed by liniment rubbed on the muscles. You'll feel like a new man."

"I'll survive." His eyes dropped from her face to the inch-high stack of letters. "I wonder why Carlton considers these our top priority."

"Customer satisfaction. Carlton's centers aren't like other emergency clinics, where a patient only drops in when he needs quick medical attention. They started out as doctor's offices in strip malls and evolved into self-contained clinics. Many of the doctors have cared for the same patients for ten or fifteen years."

Joshua shifted in his chair in an effort to get comfortable. "Why don't we read these, then organize them into piles according to the type of complaint—personnel, treatment, cost and so forth.''

Kristie sat back in her chair and gave him a hard look. He might be a fine business administrator, but he wouldn't be able to concentrate worth a damn if his legs muscles started to cramp.

He read the first letter, then glanced up at Kristie. "What's wrong?''

"We're going to have major problems working together.''

"Why?''

"Because I'm supposed to obediently follow your suggestions while you blithely ignore mine.''

"Meaning?''

"Meaning that you'll never get any work done until we do something to ease those sore muscles of yours, but you won't listen to my prescription.''

He dropped the papers on the desk and rose carefully. "You're the doctor. I'll be back in fifteen minutes.''

"I'll get the liniment.''

A mental picture of himself, naked, stretched out on a sheet, with Kristie applying liniment liberally to his backside, was enough to make him blurt, "N-no! A hot soak will suffice.''

"You really can't take doctor's orders, can you? Tell me, Joshua, if I prescribed an aspirin, would you slice it in half?'' Kristie rose, went over to the medicine cabinet and selected a muscle-relaxing ointment.

"No, but—''

She turned and began to stalk him. Her father had given him the tetanus shot she'd prescribed. She'd give him the rubdown. For some unexplainable reason, it was important to her that he accept her as a qualified physician.

"Are you a contortionist?" The red cap of the tube tapped against one of the pearlized buttons on his shirt. "Can you apply this yourself?"

"No."

He stepped backward. She stepped forward, shaking the tube in his face.

"Do you think you're my first rubdown? A medical guinea pig for Dr. Frankenstein?"

"No, but—"

"Have you ever had a rubdown?"

"Yes." And he damn well knew the result that having this woman's hands gliding sensuously up and down him would have on his libido. "I don't think it's...appropriate for you to be alone with a man who's buck naked!"

"Worried, Josh? Do you think I'm sex-starved?"

"Of course not, but . . ."

The closer she came to him, the more he was tempted to stop her sassy mouth by pulling her into his arms and planting a smoldering kiss on it. Then she could worry about him being sex-starved!

"So why are you making *but-but-but* noises? Do you think you're a Model T?"

Unamused, he raked his hand through his hair and gave her the first excuse that came to mind. "Dusty has already warned me to keep my eyes off you. He'll skin me alive if he knows you're in my bedroom with me undressed."

"I'll lock the door."

"Great! After Dusty knocks the door down he'll really be in the mood to skin me alive."

"You aren't afraid of Dusty. What's the real reason? Do you think I'm too incompetent to apply ointment to your buttocks?" She gestured with the tube toward the pile of papers. "I didn't insult you by refusing to let you read those letters."

She had him; she could tell from the grim set of his mouth.

He looked down at his wristwatch. "I'll be ready in twenty minutes."

Kristie grinned triumphantly. "I'll be there."

After he disappeared from sight, she crossed from the office to her bedroom; she wanted to take a quick shower to get the smell of horses off her skin. One look at her rumpled sheets and she began having second thoughts about going to Joshua's bedroom.

It was all well and good to salve her professional ego by insisting on rubbing liniment on Joshua's backside, but, considering her own hormonal imbalance, she'd have been wiser to prescribe her medication and let Dusty or Drew apply it.

Her eyes moved from the tangled sheets to the pills beside the sink. It was too late now to do anything about her hormones, her dreams or her lack of judgment. She'd badgered Joshua into accepting her help; she'd never be able to look him in the eye if he knew what a coward she'd turned into.

She stripped off her clothing, reached into the shower stall and turned on the cold water.

"Bubbly hot water for him and pelting ice water for me," she muttered as she reached for the soap and stepped under the spray. Her eyes went wide with shock. "Coward, hell! Only the stouthearted could endure this!"

Her body temperature plummeted. Goose bumps peppered her skin. She clamped her teeth together to keep them from chattering. When the soap refused to lather, she decided that the perfumed lump of lard and ashes was smarter than she was. She turned on the hot water.

"Ahhh," she sighed. "Better."

Along with the drastic change in water temperature came renewed control over her unruly fears. She'd reached the ripe old age of twenty-nine-and-a-half without letting her active imagination eclipse reality. She'd had plenty of opportunities to indulge in physical entanglements, but with one exception she'd avoided romantic interludes. Just as there were prerequisites for obtaining a medical degree, there were prerequisites for entering into an affair of the heart.

Love, lasting love, eternal love, the kind that made a man cherish the memory of a woman after she'd passed into the hereafter. The kind of love her father had for her mother. But, more than the love they'd shared, she mused as she lathered her legs, she wanted a love that stretched until it warmly cocooned their children, keeping them safe from the doubts that had always plagued her.

Her special requirements included as their very cornerstones trust and mutual respect. A man whom, even if all the evidence should ever point against him, she could still stand beside with her head held high. Mutual respect would keep him from betraying their love.

Kristie made a wry face as she rinsed the soap from her body. No wonder she was single. But she'd never be happy if she lowered her standards.

She hadn't avoided love, and she wouldn't. When the right time and the right man came along, she'd open her heart, reach out to him and hold on tight. If Joshua Hayden was the man . . . then so be it.

Precious minutes later, she was dry and perfumed, with her hair brushed until its sun-streaked highlights gleamed. She dressed in white slacks and a white scoop-necked top, subconsciously choosing items of the color associated with the medical profession. Her dangling gold earrings and wide navy-blue cinch belt were the only concessions she made to her femininity.

Picking up the tube of ointment, she strode toward the guest suite, refusing to continue waging mental warfare against herself. Nothing was going to happen unless she wanted it to happen!

Twenty minutes to the second from when Joshua had left the office, she knocked three times on his door.

"Come in and get it over with," Joshua said, burying his red face in his pillow.

He'd pulled the top sheet up until it covered him from head to toe. Earlier he'd shut the drapes so that only a sliver of light peeked through the locked patio door.

False modesty? Uh-uh, he thought. Sensible! Perhaps as long as he lay flat on his stomach he could conceal the impact those small hands of hers would have on him. He didn't want to respond to her, but he was prudent enough to accept the inevitable.

Kristie flipped on the light as she entered the darkened room.

"Turn off the light," Joshua muttered; the command was muffled by the pillow over his head.

Bashful *and* arrogant? Kristie grinned. The only consistency about this man was his inconsistency.

"Haven't you noticed?" she asked, locking the door to ensure their privacy. "My eyes are blue, not green cat eyes that glow in the dark." She heard him mutter something. Crossing to the side of the bed, she lifted the corner of the pillow. "I beg your pardon?"

"Periwinkle blue," Joshua shouted, loud and clear. "Turn off the damn lights!"

"Don't be ridiculous. Do you think you're the first male body I've..." She whipped back the sheet, swallowed and finished weakly, "...seen?"

Joshua heard the pause; he glanced over his shoulder and saw her blush.

She isn't totally immune to me, either, he realized. That realization fanned the flames of his imagination. He smothered a low groan with the pillow.

"My, my, what well-developed glutei maximi you have," she said, tossing out the medical term in a weak effort to conceal the very female reactions she was having. Her eyes followed the hollow of his spine to his shoulders. "Not bad deltoids and trapezoids, either."

The tube of ointment she'd been rolling between the palms of her hands to warm it was growing increasingly slippery from the dampness of her palms. She unscrewed the cap and reminded herself sternly that Joshua Hayden was a patient in need of treatment for muscular pain. She couldn't, *wouldn't*, think of him as a man.

Joshua felt his abdominal muscles contract around the multitude of butterflies batting their wings in his stomach. Why the hell had he let her talk him into treating his sore muscles? Dusty had more to worry about than his eyes following her around. Right now he should be worried about his fingers!

Between clenched teeth, he muttered, "I pumped iron a couple of times a week at the hospital employees' workout room to keep in shape."

Temporalis muscles contracting, she thought, looking at the muscles along the side of his head that clenched his teeth. She'd much rather have seen the zygomaticus and risorius muscles pull his mouth up into a smile.

"What are you waiting for—Christmas?"

His question prompted her into action. She knelt beside his hips and squirted lotion across his scapula—his shoulder blades, down his spinal column, over his gluteus maximus, and straight down his biceps femoris. Mentally listing the technical names for his muscles failed to distract her from the warmth and suppleness of his epidermis—his skin.

Her hands moved across his shoulders, massaging the unguent deep into the pores of his skin. "You're tense," she remarked, her own shoulders bunching into a mass of tight knots.

Joshua made a conscious effort to appear aloof, unaffected by the ministrations of her skilled hands. Paradoxically, however, the harder he concentrated on relaxing, the tenser he became. Beneath the pillow, his hands curled into tight fists.

She has no idea of what she's doing to me. If she did she'd run from the room screaming, he told himself. Don't think about that. Don't think about sex or anything remotely related to those topics. It's forbidden! Taboo!

While his mind worked overtime to quell his response to her fingers, his imagination worked double-time as he pictured her stroking him erotically.

She closed her eyes. Her hands unerringly followed the downward path that she'd painted with lotion. Maybe, just maybe, if she didn't look, she could perform the task from memory; maybe she could concentrate on the massage instead of the man.

"It smells like wintergreen," Joshua said gruffly to break the silence. "You said the stuff would stink."

"I fibbed."

The fib she'd told him was lily-white in comparison with the big black lie she'd been frantically repeating to herself: he's just a male patient. Her mind steadily refused to think of Joshua as a skeleton and organs covered with muscle and skin.

He was a man, all man.

He was a man she'd hated at first sight, but she couldn't force herself to believe she disliked him now. Not with the sides of her hands lightly pummelling his hard muscles.

Gradually Joshua's muscles began to respond to the treatment. The tension he'd felt began to subside, along with the dull aching pain.

"Kristine?"

"Mmm?"

His flesh was like putty in the hands of a master sculptor. Her strokes, which had been short and choppy became smooth and elongated.

"Tell me about yourself."

"What's to tell?"

"Everything. What were you like as a little kid?"

Safe territory, she thought, her eyes opening and her fingers following the indentation of his back to his shoulder blades.

"As far back as I can remember I always played nurse or doctor. While other girls changed Barbie's clothing, I changed her bandages." She grinned at the thought of the clumsy, mummylike bindings she had wrapped around her patients. "I made a general nuisance of myself tagging along with Carlton."

"Daddy's miniature Florence Nightingale, huh?"

"Yeah. More or less." Less rather than more, she mused. Carlton had been too busy starting up clinics to give her much attention. Given a choice between being left at home with Maude and listening to her father charm his patients, she'd chosen the latter. "What were you doing?"

"The usual boy stuff. Little league. Bike riding. Football. Remote-control cars."

"Sounds like a happy childhood."

"It was."

It wasn't the way she'd pictured him. A no-nonsense man should have been a no-nonsense kid. He should have told her about sticking his nose in his book so he could be the top student in class. On the other hand, the discrepancy shouldn't have surprised her. He was a man of contradictions.

Her fingers tormented the last area of resistance, at the base of his neck.

"That feels *sooo* good."

She hunched over him and whispered, "I give painless tetanus shots, too."

He chuckled softly.

He was rusty there, she mused, pleased to have made him laugh. The sound he'd just made could definitely be classified as an outright chuckle of amusement.

"Considering your happy childhood, you don't do that often."

"Laugh?" He rolled onto his back, pulling the sheet to his waist in a single, lithe movement as he did so. "Of course I do."

Her hands followed his until they rested motionless on his chest. "Oh, yeah? In your sleep? When you're tickled?"

Before her fingers could dart to the nest of hair under his arm, Joshua grabbed her wrist. His dark eyes brimmed with contained mirth. "I'm not ticklish."

"Then why'd you stop me?" Her fingers waggled in front of his face. "Now who's fibbing?"

"I confess. I'm a *little* ticklish."

"Tough guy, huh? Won't admit he squirms like a worm when tickled. You're impossible, Joshua Hayden. Utterly impossible."

"Oh, I'm possible, Dr. Kristine." He tugged on her upper arm until her elbows unlocked and her forearms fell against his chest. Her lips were scant inches from his. "I'm possible, not impossible."

She shouldn't, she knew she shouldn't, but her mouth couldn't resist tasting the flavor of the smile he so seldom used. She had wanted to kiss him earlier. Now it seemed imperative. As her lips came closer to his, she looked into his eyes and saw desire burning bright in the dark centers and knew he wanted it, too. She kissed him, lightly. His lips tasted sweeter than she'd imagined, too sweet for her to linger there. She lifted her mouth fractionally.

"I shouldn't have done that." She tried to make light of the kiss by adding, "Kissing the patient isn't part of making a home visit."

"I'm cured. No aches. No pains." He punctuated his short sentences with nibbles on her lower lip. "I haven't been your patient since I turned over."

"It's wrong."

"It feels right."

"Only for the moment." She whispered the warning, her lips moving against his, unable to move away from him. "We'll both regret it later."

At the hint that she might leave him, his arm circled her waist to stop her. His lips quirked into a sensuous smile. He pulled her down until she lay on top of him. "I'll regret it if you leave now or later. I'm in dire need of a doctor."

"Go to a clinic," she said teasingly, peppering a line of kisses along the hard ridge of his jaw.

"You, Dr. Kristine. Just any doctor won't do." His hands stroked from her tiny waist to the ripe, womanly fullness of her hips, pressing her into the cradle of his pelvis. "I want you. I need you. I haven't wanted or needed any woman the way I want and need you. I'm hoping those feelings are mutual."

The rush of heat his candid confession brought to her cheeks raced downward, enveloping her in a flash fire of desire.

Kristie could neither agree nor disagree. His mouth captured hers in a silent, passionate plea. His tongue parted her lips, swirling inside her, obliterating any impulse to refuse him. The warning bell that usually jangled when a man came too close, too fast, had been rendered temporarily defunct.

She rocked her hips slowly against him, unashamed of the effect she had on him. With only a thin sheet and her clothing separating them, she had little doubt that he did truly want her.

Kristie had experienced wanting a man, but she'd never indulged her curiosity about the human sex drive beyond a brief, torrid affair during medical school. She'd found sex pleasurable and momentarily gratifying, but lacking the vital ingredient of love that brought a lasting afterglow. She'd reached for what she thought would lead to happiness, and she'd come up empty-handed. So she had sworn then to wait until she found what she wanted.

"Joshua, no." She levered her forearm against his chest to pry herself from his arms. "No. I mean it."

"Because you think I'm usurping your job?"

"No." She shook her head. Then she paused, remembering how he'd been hired without anyone consulting her. "Maybe." Then: "Yes!"

Her confused reply earned her a hug. His laughter, lighter and stronger than before, resounded in her ear. "Which?"

"Yes! A definite yes! I'm a partner. I should have been consulted."

Confident that he could overcome her reluctance to have him on the payroll once he had a chance to prove his worth, he clamped his arms around her waist. "Carlton was supposed to discuss the agreement with you before I arrived. His silence wasn't my fault. It certainly didn't affect what has happened since then. That's an excuse, Kristine, not the reason."

She wilted against his massive chest. "We hardly know one another."

"You want to know about those hellish years between innocent childhood and now?" His hold loosened, but his desire for her still had him in a death grip. "They don't affect you."

"You've been married. Divorced. You've fought a custody battle for your son," she said. "Doesn't any of that affect me?"

His lips were pressed together tightly. The flames in his dark eyes began to dwindle. Wanting and needing are fleeting things, she thought, and disappointment caused a sharp pang of regret to pierce her heart.

"Don't mistake my silence for lack of wanting or needing you." His hand cupped her face; his fingers wove through her fair hair. "I could weave a pitiful tale of marrying too young, for the wrong reasons, and discovering the mistake after Drew was born. That's the standard tale of woe a man in the throes of passion tells a woman, isn't it?"

"Yes." *Tell me sweet, loving lies. Make me believe them!*

She winced when his fingers tangled in her hair. His eyes lingered on her face, but she knew he wouldn't make excuses or false promises.

Silently he damned himself for the mistakes he'd made in his early twenties. He'd believed Vicky loved him; he'd learned she'd been more enchanted by the idea of a June wedding than by him. He'd believed she wanted his child; he'd learned her reasons for wanting a baby were equally shallow—her girlfriends were pregnant or had small babies. He'd thought wrong. Love had not been the motive behind Vicky's marriage or motherhood. He'd merely been the man who could provide the monthly paycheck that financed her keeping up with her friends. He'd been convenient.

Vicky's parents had besmirched the small amount of love Vicky had felt for him by twisting the ugly truth, that she didn't love him, into an even uglier lie, that he didn't love her. Because her love was frail, his wife had chosen to believe them.

Hell, the Van Horns' testimony at the divorce proceedings had almost convinced *him* of his unworthiness! It had taken years to overcome his self-doubts, to raise his self-esteem high enough to risk falling in love again.

Maybe it was best for Kristie to think the worst of him. Lies couldn't be used as a weapon against him if she heard them from his lips. He wanted her to trust him even when the evidence was damning.

If she cared, truly cared, surely she would somehow sense that he was twisting the truth.

His mouth barely moved as he said, "She had money and social position, and I was a workaholic who worshiped the almighty dollar. The perfect match."

"An opportunist," she said, quoting Drew. She felt a small tremor of apprehension. Was history repeating itself? She was part-owner of the clinics. Doctors did have prestige in the community. She satisfied the same requirements that had previously led Joshua up the aisle.

"Drew's grandparents compiled and documented a lengthy list of my personality flaws. They're a matter of public record in Boston's city courthouse."

"What isn't in the records?" She didn't want to hear their accusations. She wanted to hear his reasons.

He focused his eyes on her. "I won't whitewash what happened, Kristie. Misplaced trust is a shortcut to hell. I won't justify what happened by telling you there were extenuating circumstances. No excuses."

He'd didn't want her to feel sorry for him. Pity repelled him; it would gnaw at his self-esteem until he came to believe he was worthless again. He'd earned his self-respect, the hard way—by facing the Van Horns in that courtroom and refuting their lies. No more shortcuts. No more following the path of least resistance. Kristie had to care enough to believe in him. He'd been hurt too badly to settle for less.

Kristie didn't know what to make of what she'd heard. He'd revealed what other men would have hidden, or at least disguised with half-truths. As he'd given her his brutal account of what had happened, he'd seemed to lack the qualities she'd sensed in him when he'd saved Drew from being injured: love and compassion.

"Did you love her?"

He released her and folded his arms behind his head, lacing his fingers together; he wanted her to be able to leave if she chose. "What has love got to do with a marriage of convenience?"

Kristie would never know that those were his ex-wife's words, not his own.

"Would it be convenient for you to marry me?" Kristie asked in a small voice, her own insecurities surfacing. "Carlton said it would."

She held her breath, waiting for his answer.

No! Only an idiot buys a second ticket to hell, he thought. Carlton hadn't been to hell and back. His wife had loved him. What Joshua felt for Kristie had nothing to do with her father's clinics or with his money. But fear that her father might use the phrase *marriage of convenience*, as the Van Horns had during the custody battle over Drew, made Joshua clench his teeth and answer "Yes."

Five

A doctor relied on instincts; Kristie trusted hers.

Joshua had confronted her with hard, unqualified statements. But like X rays and blood tests, those statements could mislead a physician into prescribing the wrong medication. She had the gut feeling that there was more to Joshua Hayden than a greedy opportunist.

His dark, soulful eyes beckoned to her to look deeper, below the shallow surface of how others had interpreted his actions. He wasn't the ruthless man he'd scornfully depicted. His eyes contradicted his mouth.

She had to trust her instincts and risk being dead wrong.

Of their own volition, her fingers splayed through the mass of dark hairs on his chest until one hand covered his heart. His ribs expanded as he caught his breath and held it.

She kissed him, once, twice, until his lips parted and she felt the breath he'd been holding fan her cheeks.

"You don't care?" he asked, not quite willing to believe his good fortune.

"Oh, I care." She smiled at the tingling sensation she felt when he unlocked his hands and held her close to his heart. "I care."

Though every cell in his body was screaming for him to cling to her, he knew he had to give her one last chance to get up and walk out of his room, his pride intact. He wanted her to have the chance he'd been denied. His ex-wife had selfishly clung to him, smothering him, even when she had no longer wanted or needed him. He couldn't do that to Kristine.

His hand trembled as it tucked a stray lock of hair behind her ear. "Caring for me could be a big mistake."

"So sue me for malpractice," she crooned against his lips. "I'll take my chances."

"I want you, Kristine." The words were an impatient rasp. "But if it's still too soon I can wait."

"I can't."

His arms closed around her with rough gentleness. His rusty chuckle delighted her as he said, "One of us has on too much clothing."

Gently, he traced the ribbing of the scoop-necked blouse until his fingers touched the top button. One by one, as though they had all the time in the world, he worked the buttons open. She pulled her shirttail from her slacks, shivering in anticipation when his knuckles brushed against the soft swell of her breast.

A snap, a zipper, a shimmy of her shoulders and a tug on her slacks later, the only barrier between them was her lacy underwear. He rolled onto his side, taking her with him. For a long moment he just held her close to him, until he could gain control of the unruly urge to satisfy his hunger by taking her hard and fast.

Kristie arched against him; her arms circled his neck. She knew he was struggling to gain control, and she felt a fierce joy at the knowledge that she could break his iron will simply by rotating her hips against him. When he unclasped the clasp at the back of her bra, removed it and circled her nipple between his thumb and forefinger, she realized that he had the same power over her.

A low moan of pleasure hissed from between her lips. The slow movements of his hands were in sharp contrast to the ragged pace of his breathing. She knew he was wild with need, and yet he cared enough to want her fully aroused.

His lips left a hot, moist trail of liquid fire from the pulse point on her neck to the peak of her breast. His tongue curled around the dusty-pink crest, pulling it deep inside the hot furnace of his mouth, sucking slowly, sweetly, until her short fingernails sank into the supple flesh of his back. He kneaded her other breast, preparing it for the savage sweetness of his tongue and his teeth.

An unfamiliar tightness coiled low in her stomach.

She knew with absolute certainty that he would make this exquisite torture last forever unless she did something drastic to break his control.

She reached for him.

Joshua's eyelids snapped open when her small fingers closed around him. He muttered her name hoarsely and caught her slender wrist. "Don't."

"I want to touch you."

"Not there." Her wrist was stronger than he'd expected. Her fingers traversed the length of him until they reached the velvet tip. Lazily she traced the same pattern he'd drawn on her breast with his tongue. He muffled his low groan of pleasure in the valley between her breasts. "This won't last long enough for you if—"

"If you don't stop driving me crazy?" She needed him; she ached to please him as thoroughly as he pleased her.

He released his slack hold on her wrist; he teased the lacy edge of her bikini panties, then slid his palms down her hips, pushing the remainder of her clothing to her ankles and off his bed.

"Am I driving you crazy?" The heel of his hand settled snugly in the intimate triangle of darker blond curls at the apex of her thighs. "Tell me you want me."

Without a moment's hesitation she gasped, "I want you, Joshua."

"Not yet, little one." He shifted his hips out of her reach. Her shoulders raised, she nipped his earlobe to punish him for depriving her of the chance to give him equal treatment. He rotated his hand until small cries of ecstasy accompanied its circular movement. "Not yet, but soon, little one, soon. Don't hold back. Show me how much you need to feel me inside you."

Her hips arched and her thighs parted. Instantly he rewarded her by gliding his finger into the tangled thatch, parting her, discovering her intimate secrets.

Kristie felt faint. Her breathing became more labored with every questing thrust he made. Her hands made frantic passes across his shoulders and down his back, urging his hips toward hers.

Suddenly the world spun beneath her. Her eyes blinked open. She'd been too engrossed in breasting the waves of ecstasy that were about to claim her. She didn't know how it had happened, but she was straddled on top of him, her knees on either side of his hips.

He lifted her face from his chest. Their eyes met—hers bewildered and clouded with passion, his confident in the knowledge that he'd brought her to the edge without taking her beyond.

Slowly his hips moved beneath her. The spiralling ache became almost painful as he denied her the only thing that could relieve it.

His smoldering eyes challenged her. "Want me?"

"Please."

He issued a final demand, in a voice heavily laden with desire: "You'll have to take me."

She lifted her hips; her shoulders cast his face in shadow as she slowly settled on the length of him. He's letting me dominate him, she mused. Why?

He came into her with a boldness that made her have second thoughts about who was dominating whom. Her nails raked his chest as he filled her completely, leaving no doubt as to who was in command. She adjusted her rhythm to his. It was like riding a wild bronco, and yet it was very different. She locked her knees beside his driving hips, thrilling to the powerful feel of his muscular body.

Nothing she'd ever experienced had prepared her for these uplifting, soaring sensations. With each thrust he took her to new heights. His hands were all over her, caressing her arms, her waist, her breasts, her thighs.

He brought her mouth to his. He nibbled, laved, then thrust deep into the sweet cavern of her mouth, just when he arched his hips inches off the bed.

Joshua Hayden made love as though there were no tomorrows, no yesterdays. Only here. Only now. Only Kristine.

"Joshua?" Her insides constricted, pulsating, throbbing, relaxing, then clenching him harder.

"Don't hold back. Give yourself to me," he demanded. His short breaths panted against her skin; his steely control slipped when he witnessed the expression of complete amazement on her face. He saw her go completely taut above him, her head flung back, her thighs a vise around him. "Say my name."

"Joshua . . . Joshua . . . Joshua."

He could hardly hear the sound of his name on her lips above the roaring in his ears as he exploded inside her. She was his; he was hers. Together they'd achieved the impossible—they'd become one.

His heart pumped bubbles of pure joy through his veins. As they percolated through him, a low rumble of laughter that started in his chest slowly built until it burst across his tongue and between his lips.

Collapsed across him, Kristie raised her head in wonderment. There was no mistaking the sound—it was sheer happiness. Her lips responded by lifting into a satisfied smile. She knew deep inside that she'd given him something special. With her he could. love and laugh without restraint.

His lips curved upward as he peppered tiny hot kisses across her cheeks. All he could think to say was "Thank you, little one, from the bottom of my heart, thank you."

Dreamily she asked, "No complaints?"

"Only one. I wish those sensations could have lasted forever."

She tweaked a strand of his chest hair, then faked a look of disappointment and slithered to his side. "Are you telling me they can't?"

"Lady, you're the doctor. What would happen if our hearts maintained that rate of speed indefinitely?"

Kristie paused, loving the teasing quality in his voice, loving the sight of his eyes lit with good humor. "A massive coronary thrombosis?"

"A heart attack." His finger traced the bow of her lips. His dark eyes became serious. "You have attacked my heart, little one. From the moment I saw you crossing the side yard, with your face smudged, your chin tilted upward, I felt a tug on my heartstrings."

She nipped at his finger. "You hid it well. I'd never have guessed. Knowing what I know now...how contradictory you are...I should have realized that beneath that cool aloof exterior was a man—" she grinned to take the sting from her words "—lusting after me."

"Not lust at first sight. I thought you were Drew's age. The lust didn't come until you shook my hand." One of his hands trailed over her waist and hip. With regret, he added, "Speaking of Drew..."

Kristie sighed. "I feel like a kid who just heard the recess bell ring. Time to stop playing around and get back to work, hmmm?"

He lowered his mouth to hers for one last taste of her. His kiss held a promise of more good things to come... later.

"Later," Joshua muttered, pushing the ledgers she'd placed on the desk farther away from him. Thoughts of her, naked, stretched out beside him on the bed, kept interfering with the work piled in front of him. He leaned back in Carlton's chair and rubbed his forehead in total exasperation. "I'm going to be up all night tackling these letters. I can't believe there are four letters from a man with chronic gout. Why isn't he going to a regular doctor?''

She grinned. ''By regular, do you mean certified?''

''You know what I mean. Why doesn't he go to the same doctor every time?''

''If he goes on a regular basis to the same clinic, we try to match him to the same doctor on every visit.''

''According to his letters, he's been to three different doctors at three different clinics. All the man wants is to have his prescription renewed, but every time the doctor runs blood tests. He thinks the clinics are unjustifiably racking up his bill with laboratory expenses.'' He shoved the letters toward her. ''Why weren't any of his letters answered?''

''That's Dad's department.'' An impish smile teased her lips. She wondered what Joshua would do if she came around the desk and plopped herself down in his lap. ''I guess he got a little behind while he was recovering from his heart attack.''

''A little behind? Why a patient continues to come to the clinic when he thinks he's being ripped off is beyond me. I'd have gone elsewhere.'' He picked up the first letter and tossed it across the desk. ''Read the date.''

''The tenth of June.''

''Of last year!''

''Carlton felt tired and listless long before he was rushed to the hospital.'' Both blood and business ties to her father made Kristie defensive about his negligence. It wasn't as though the man had gone without his medicine. Didn't Joshua realize that when he criticized her father's oversights he was also hurting her? She had never been able to control Carlton, but that didn't stop her from feeling partially responsible. She was a partner, after all. "Why don't we just dictate a nice letter of apology and refund the charges for the blood tests?"

"And what happens the next time this man's prescription needs to be filled."

"We'll put a note in his file that he's only to be tested annually."

"Which file? Which clinic? From what I can gather, there must not be any communication between the clinics. Are they run like separate doctors' offices?"

"They operate independently of one another. Dad didn't want the clinics to be operated like a string of fast-food restaurants—'Doc in the Boxes.' He wanted to maintain the individual integrity of each clinic."

Joshua flung one arm in the air and gestured toward the door. "The name in neon lights outside the clinic is the same, but the patients are treated like strangers every time they walk through the door?"

His sarcasm made her bristle. "We know that's a problem. We tried mailing copies of records to each branch. You know how reliable the mail is—not to mention the expense of hiring extra staff to file the records or buying a multitude of filing cabinets to house the records. It was more expedient for the patient to take five minutes and fill out another form." She shoved the sheet of paper across the table, literally dumping the problems back in his lap. "There is a blank at the bottom of the form that asks if the patient has received treatment at another one of our clinics. Obviously Mr. Chronic Gout didn't fill it in properly."

"If the receptionist saw that the blank was empty, would she inquire about it?"

Kristie shrugged. "Maybe. Maybe not. That would depend on whether or not the waiting room was jam-packed, full of other emergency cases."

"I know this is a dumb question, but I'll ask it for the sake of enlightenment. Is there a written manual of policies and procedures for office help?"

"No."

"The secretaries and clerks just come in and do their thing—loosey-goosey?"

"We've managed without written rules and regulations. Each year the business has grown," she replied stiffly, battling to keep a scalpel-sharp response from leaping impetuously from her mouth. The unanswered letters were Carlton's fault, but hiring and overseeing the clerical staff had been her job for several years.

"No thanks to the efficiency of this organization," he muttered, folding his arms over his chest. "You and your father are lucky central Florida's population is growing by leaps and bounds."

"Or we're fortunate that most of our patients have the sense to use the same center each time."

"Do you have any statistics on how many patients seek medical care elsewhere?" Joshua hunched over the desk again. His thumb riffled through the corners of the letters stacked in front of him. "None of these people are very pleased."

Kristie had had enough of this inquisition. She planted the flat of her hand on the desk and arched her hand across his neatly stacked papers.

"What are you doing?"

"Looking for something." She picked up one pile, pretended to look under it, then pitched the papers into the air. While the letters fluttered to the carpet, she reached for the next stack. When Joshua flattened his arms on top of the remaining papers to keep her from wreaking more havoc, she felt like hitting him so hard that when he woke up his clothes would be outdated!

"Ask if you're looking for something, would you? You're deliberately making a mess."

"Okay!" Her nose was an inch from his. She barely managed to keep her voice at a conversational level. "Tell me, Joshua, since you have everything in its proper pigeonhole, where'd you put the man who made love with me less than two hours ago? I can't find him anywhere."

Realizing he'd been a little hard on her, he reached toward her. She straightened and backed away from him.

"C'mon, Kristine." He rose from the chair and circled the desk. "You're taking this personally. You don't have to be defensive about mismanaging—"

"Mismanaging!"

Again he tried to close the yawning gap between them by reaching for her. "*Mismanagement* was a poor choice of words. Nothing has been done that I can't rectify. If this upsets you, I can straighten things out on my own."

She avoided his grasp by sidestepping and moving back.

"Don't you patronize me by patting me on the head and telling me to run along while you straighten out the mess I've made."

He could tell by the mulish expression on her face that she wasn't going to listen to reason. Shoving his hands in his pockets, he turned toward the window overlooking the corral.

Kristine stood frozen in place, wondering what he expected her to do. He'd turned his back and walked away from her. Was she supposed to wait until he hurled another criticism in her face? It was pointless to remind Joshua that it was Carlton who had filed the letters and forgotten them. Was he standing there like a statue because he was waiting for her to pick up the papers she'd scattered on the carpet?

Not in this decade, she mused, stepping backward. He specialized in cleaning up business messes. Let him do it!

She felt the doorknob pressing against her back. He can stand there until doomsday, she decided. Silently, she opened the door and walked out.

Frustrated by his inept handling of the situation, Joshua pinched the bridge of his nose to keep her light floral scent from distracting him. He had to stop thinking of her as a woman and start thinking of her as a business associate!

Business was business. Facts were facts. The clinics had been mismanaged! Since Carlton had conveniently disappeared, she was his one link to the clinics. To streamline the clinics he had to ask questions she preferred not to answer.

Kristine resented the fact that her father made business decisions without checking with her, and yet here she was in a tizzy because he'd calmly pointed out the deficiencies in the present organizational setup.

Her suggestions that they refund the patient's money was like prescribing a couple of aspirin for a man with gallstones. It might make the patient feel better temporarily, but it wouldn't solve the underlying problem.

Drastic changes had to be made. He wanted her to willingly take part in those changes. He'd been right to cut through the flab and get to the heart of the problem.

Then why was he feeling like an executioner?

A meaningless apology would taste sour in his mouth. He wanted to pacify Kristine at any cost. But the moment he opened his mouth and apologized for stating what he believed was right he'd lose her respect. She'd consider him a wishy-washy wimp she could boss around.

He could apologize for the way he'd presented the facts to her; he couldn't apologize for the truth.

"I should have been more tactful. I'm sorry," he said. When there was no reply, he turned around.

The office was empty.

Outside the door, Kristie was tapping her foot impatiently, none too pleased with her unprofessional behavior. She should have known that making excuses for Carlton's not having answered the letters wouldn't work with Joshua. He was a man who neither made excuses for his own actions nor accepted excuses for the actions of others.

She'd been defensive about her father's oversights. Her defensiveness had quickly changed to hostility when Joshua had asked about a manual of policies and procedures for the clerks. That was her concern, and his question cut close to the bone. It had never occurred to her to present new employees with a manual. Courtesy and common sense—those were the things she stressed.

She had to admit that the office staff were laid-back. But loosey-goosey? Yeah, she mused, that too. Where had Joshua, an uptight, tight-lipped, persnickety Bostonian, gotten that expression?

The answer to her question came careening out of the kitchen and ran down the hallway toward her. He dropped down on one leg, as if he were skidding into home plate. Dusting off his threadbare pant leg, he said, "Are you and Joshua—uh, Dad—are you guys finished? I don't wanna get my head bitten off for bothering him while he's busy, but I gotta ask him something real important?''

"A life-and-death matter?" She was tempted to ruffle his hair. Without his lip curled into a snarl, Joshua's son had a boyish appeal that she found irresistible. "You can't wait until dinner to ask?"

"I could, but I've got a kid waitin' on me for an answer." His face turned tomato red, and his gaze dropped to the toes of his running shoes. "You know Jenny Lynn Baxter, from down the road? Well, her parents are taking her to Disney World tomorrow and she asked me if I can go."

"What about school? Monday isn't a holiday."

"Nope. It's a teacher's workday. You know, when they work on report cards or go to meetings. Lucky for me, huh?" He glanced over his shoulder. "She's waiting. I guess if Dad's busy...since I'm staying here at your house, I could get permission from you." Drew grabbed for her hand.

"Oh, no, you don't," Kristie said. "I went against your father's wishes when I let you ride Lazy Bones yesterday, remember? That didn't work out the way you planned. You're my guest, but you're his son."

"You could ask 'em for me. Please!"

"Uh-uh." She knocked on the door, then opened it. "You do your own asking."

"What's going on?" Joshua crossed to the door, where Drew had latched on to Kristie's arm and was pulling her toward him.

"Kristine wants to ask you something," Drew said.

"Drew wants to ask you something," Kristie said at the same time.

"You first," they both chorused, pointing at each other. "No, you first."

"Hold it!" Joshua raised both hands. "Drew?"

"Okay, okay!" Drew muttered, hooking his thumbs in his back pockets. "There's no school tomorrow and I've been invited by the kid down the road to go to Disney World."

Joshua had been looking forward to taking Drew there, but he sensed that his son badly wanted to go with the neighbors. "I don't see any problems with your going with him."

"Her," Kristie said, ignoring the dirty look Drew sent her. "Jenny Lynn Baxter, to be exact. Her parents are friends of ours."

"Can I go, Dad? Please?"

"You'll be careful?"

"Yeah! I promise!"

"Kristine, we're *your* guests," Joshua said, anxious to include her in the decision-making process. "Do you have any objections?"

She shook her head, pleased at having been consulted.

"Whoopee!" Drew impulsively hugged Kristie and then his father. "Thanks! I'm gonna go tell Jenny it's okay!"

Drew's elation must have been contagious. Kristie found herself grinning at Joshua.

He returned her smile. "Puppy love?"

"Spring fever," Joshua countered, inching toward her. "It seems to be in the air around here."

Warmth from the smoldering heat in his eyes burned her cheeks. "I guess I owe you an apology for messing up your work."

"Apology accepted." His arms circled her. Against the silkiness of her hair he whispered, "And I owe you one for being undiplomatic."

She raised herself up on tiptoe, kicked the door shut and linked her arms behind his neck. "Accepted."

"I want to work with you."

Kristie grinned. From the feel of the hand urgently pressing her against him she guessed he wanted more than a working partnership. She wasn't about to argue about it.

His head lowered. Her lips parted, ready to receive a kiss to seal the pact.

"Someone is coming," he whispered with a sigh of regret, the kindling fire lighting the depths of his dark eyes instantly doused. "It could be Drew."

Her fingers trekked down his arms as he withdrew from her.

A frown of puzzlement drew her brows together. Was Joshua going to hide whatever it was he felt for her from his son? She knew he wanted to keep Drew's life uncomplicated until the boy adjusted to his new surroundings, but did he consider her a complication? She searched his face for signs of guilt or shame. His expression was unreadable; he'd pulled an impenetrable mask over his emotions.

"You're going to have to stop doing that ... hiding your feelings," she cautioned. "It's a stress-builder."

Joshua's slow, sexy wink caught her totally off guard and erased her frown. She'd opened her mouth to issue another dire medical edict, and now she snapped it shut. His eyes flickered with barely concealed amusement.

"What's so damn funny?"

"The thought of you and me in a mad, passionate clutch, with Drew on the sidelines scribbling notes. Twelve-year-old boys are extremely curious about the birds and bees, especially when they've been raised in a household where hugging and kissing were taboo."

"Oh." Kristine swallowed, remembering that Drew didn't seem to know the difference between a mare and a stallion. "No sex education classes taught in the Boston schools?"

Joshua chuckled dryly and shook his head. "Only with parental permission."

Three sharp raps on the door and the sound of Maude calling her name prevented Kristie from exploring this subject further.

"Yes, Maude?" she asked, opening the door.

The rotund, gray-haired housekeeper swished past Kristie and waddled straight toward Joshua. "Drew wanted to know if it was okay for him to eat dinner at the Baxters' house. I told him he could, as long as he watched his manners and was back here before dark."

From the pugnacious tone of her voice and the battle gleam in her brown eyes Kristie knew Drew had found a supporter, an I'm-on-your-side-kid go-between. Like her husband, Maude took liberties only a valued employee dared to take. Joshua was in for a tussle if he tried to overrule Maude's authority.

"Thanks," Joshua said simply.

Maude blinked, taken aback by his easy capitulation. "He didn't think you'd let him go."

"I trust your judgment." When he felt Kristie's eyes boring into him, he added, "I hadn't told him not to eat at Jennifer's house the way I'd explicitly told him to stay off the horses."

"He figured you'd hold up dinner around here 'cause you're holed up in here. Kristie'll tell you, when meals are fixed, I expect you to be there."

"And she expects you to clean your plate," Kristie said sweetly.

"Last night's tuna-fish casserole had Drew eating double helpings. I've had a real problem getting him to eat green vegetables, though. Do you think—?"

Maude primped the coiled knot of hair at her nape. "Smother 'em in oregano. Makes 'em think they're eating pizza." She patted Joshua on the arm. "Don't you worry none about that boy eatin' right, Mr. Joshua. I'll have Drew fat and sassy in no time."

"I can't tell you how much you've relieved my mind, Maude."

Maude waved a dismissive hand, harrumphed and turned toward the kitchen. The look she gave Kristie was stamped with approval for her houseguest.

It took great restraint on Kristie's part to keep from rolling her eyes and making a face at Maude's acceptance of Joshua's blatant flattery. A few seconds after the door closed she murmured quietly, "She'll have us all eating spinach by this time next week—and loving it."

"Spinach with oregano?" Joshua's grimace was a carbon copy of his son's when tuna-fish casserole had been mentioned. "Do you think I could convince her grown men don't eat spinach?"

"I'd say that if that's possible you'd be the one to do it. She's pretty taken with you. I halfway expected her to take the pins from her hair and ruffle it loose. Or unbutton the collar of that prim dress of hers. Did you notice how her hips swayed when she left the room?" Kristie pointed at the smug grin plastered on his face. "You, Mr. Hayden, have an adverse effect on a determined woman's intent to scold you unmercifully."

"Does it work on you?"

A slow smile curved her lips. Her hips swaying provocatively she advanced on him. "I'm tougher than Maude."

She was in his arms with his lips next to her ear when he whispered, "For you, I'd eat bushels of spinach . . . without the oregano."

Six

Nine days. Eleven hours. Twenty-seven minutes. That was how long it had been since Joshua had touched her. She'd considered going to him. Actually, she'd done more than think about it. Yesterday she'd gone to the guest suite, prepared to beat on the door—and his chest, if necessary—to find out why he was keeping her at arm's length. Through the door she'd heard the sounds of Joshua and Drew roughhousing—squeals of delight from Drew, laughing threats from Joshua. Much as she'd wanted to be a part of their fun, she'd retreated to her room.

Was Drew the reason behind Joshua's chastity? Joshua had mentioned that his son had been raised in an emotionally sterile environment. Surely holding her hand or giving her a peck on the check wouldn't throw Drew into an emotional tizzy. Of course Joshua wanted

Drew to feel secure, but did he think showing affection toward her would be perceived by Drew as a threat?

She'd be worried if Drew didn't like her, but that wasn't the case. When he wasn't at school or with Joshua or Jenny Lynn he was with her. Not counting the hours when she was working with Joshua, she spent as much time with Drew as she did with his father.

Her deep-seated insecurity reared its ugly head. Was Joshua purposely excluding her by not informing Drew of their relationship? She peeked at the man seated at the computer terminal.

He hadn't excluded her from the decision-making process at work.

Her prediction that he'd be given a strong dose of laughing gas by the clinic's employees had been entirely incorrect. She was the only person who'd been ill-tempered and out of sorts. He'd beguiled everyone! He had everybody in the house eating Maude's spinach balls, for heaven's sake.

"A GOMER just arrived," Dr. Reid Warner said, sticking his head in the door of Kristie's office at the Winter Park clinic. "Burns."

Kristie hastily shrugged into her lab jacket without giving Joshua the second lingering look that she usually cast in his direction before leaving the cramped office they shared.

He punched the Save button on the computer and followed her. The first time he'd heard an intern shout the acronym for Get Out Of My Emergency Room, at the start of his career as a hospital administrator, it had signaled the arrival of six teenagers involved in a grisly automobile accident.

Reid had the small, whimpering child on a stretcher and was wheeling him to an examining room. Detaining him by touching his arm, Kristine told him to get the information they needed from the glassy-eyed woman trailing along behind the stretcher.

"Velma, get a morphine sulfate IV started," Kristie told the nurse who was helping put the little boy on the examination table. Her practiced eyes moved over him as she checked his pulse. Her first concern was to make certain the child wasn't in shock; then she'd administer medication to relieve his pain and combat fluid loss.

Some fast thinker must have removed his clothing before it could adhere to the wound, she thought, grateful to the stranger.

She checked for respiratory distress and began to silently assess the injury. Front of trunk. Twenty percent. First- and second-degree. Closed treatment. It wasn't as bad as it could have been. She'd seen worse.

"You're going to be fine, big fella," she murmured, certain that only the epidermis and the corium were involved. "We're going to take good care of you."

"Mommy?"

"She's right outside."

His eyelids drooped heavily. "The ouchie doesn't hurt so bad now."

Kristie glanced up at the clear fluid that was dripping steadily from the bottle overhead. Certain that enough medication had been administered to keep the child comfortable, she began washing the injury with the antibacterial soap and water Velma gave her.

Reid entered the room. He began assisting Kristie by checking the child's vital signs, speaking sotto voce. "Mrs. Gunther and her kids were shopping. Just as they passed the food counter, Bobby's eight-year-old sister tried to keep him from running down the aisle by picking him up. He squirmed, kicking and flinging his arms around. His sister let go just as he knocked a coffeepot off the burner. One of the waitresses saw what happened, dunked him in a sink of cold water and stripped off his clothing.''

"That lady probably saved him from third-degree burns. How are the mother and sister?''

"Badly shaken up. Both blaming themselves for the accident. A couple of weeks ago I did a thyroid workup on Mrs. Gunther. Since we're closer than the hospital, she brought him here.''

"He's going to need a tetanus toxoid booster. Silver sulfadiazine, gentamicin sulfate ointments.'' Feeling a draft, Kristie glanced up and saw Joshua slip into the room. "Keep the door closed. We don't want any drafts in here until I have him bandaged.''

Joshua nodded. He knew he would be more of a hindrance than a help; he wasn't sure what had compelled him to enter the examining room. The silent communication between the doctors and the nurse—a nod, a raised hand, a frown—excluded him completely.

"What do you think, Kristine?'' Reid asked, pinching the red thread at the corner of a Texas-size bandage harder than was necessary to open the sterile gauze. The look he gave Joshua clearly read GOMER!

Momentarily distracted by Joshua's presence, Kristie grunted, "Huh?''

"Do you think the boy has to be hospitalized?''

She watched the steady rising and falling of the boy's chest. "He needs fluid replacement therapy, and he'll need watching, though he seems stable.'' She distributed the ointment lightly on the boy's chest. "Velma, would you call over to the hospital and have them send an ambulance? Make the other necessary arrangements, too.''

Joshua heard the soft request, but his eyes were focused on the transparent gloves she was wearing on her hands. In the past ten days, he'd become fascinated by them. He'd noticed them when they'd been introduced, when she'd gripped his hand and instantly changed his mind about her age, he'd noticed them. Small but capable; gentle but assured; fragile and yet strong. They could rein in a skittish horse ten times her size, snap a pencil in half when she was irritated, permanently pleat the front of her skirt when she was nervous or flutter beguilingly across his face to incite him to a frenzy of passion. And now, just as naturally, her agile fingers were applying ointment to heal a child's wounds.

He was completely under the spell her hands were weaving. It was as if she were a miracle worker, as if she could simply lay those small, womanly hands on his chest and thaw the block of ice surrounding his heart. Right now, all she'd have to do was look up at him and crook one little finger in his direction and his heart would skip a beat, then pump heated blood straight to his libido, thawing the ice water in his veins.

''Careful,'' Kristie said to Reid, making certain the bandage they were wrapping around the child's torso was applied with uniform pressure. A mere flick of her finger told her associate that the exterior gauze on top of the bandage was too tight. When the final piece of tape was attached to the gauze, she grinned at the little boy and said, ''You are one brave little fella.''

Bobby smiled weakly. ''*Big* fella.''

''Too big to pick a toy from the cabinet?''

Bobby's china-blue eyes brightened, and his blond head rocked from side to side. "Do big boys with big ouchies get big toys?"

"Good things come in little packages—like you and me! I'm sure I'll find something special in here that you'll like."

Kristie peeled off her disposable surgical gloves, rolled back the stool she'd been perched on and opened a cabinet stocked with new toys. A meaningful glance from Reid to the door told him that he should go tell the child's mother about his condition and give her their recommendation that he be hospitalized overnight.

Both Bobby's and Joshua's eyes followed her. Bobby was expecting a toy; Joshua was anticipating something far, far more pleasant. He ached for a long, lingering kiss once they were alone.

"Ah-ha! What's this?" Kristie pulled out a Matchbox racing car that fitted easily in the palm of the boy's hand. "It's special, because the hood and the trunk and the doors open."

"Oh, boy," Bobby whispered, trying to open all of them at once. "Can I have it for keeps?"

"Sure. Oh, look! There's something that goes with the car." She pulled out a stick-and-paste book about cars and a yellow ramp with a trigger pull.

"What's that?"

Joshua crossed to the boy's side. "You put the back wheels of the car in here and pull the trigger and the car races off the ramp." He let Bobby position the car, then crouched down and fired the trigger. The racing car zoomed across the room. "See? You'll have to wait until you're up and around before you can play with it, but in the meantime you can stick racing stripes on the cars in the picture book."

Bobby glanced from his arm to the IV bottle hanging from the rack, and asked Joshua, "Doctor, where's my mom?"

"Here I am, sweetheart." Hesitantly his mother entered the room, obviously distressed by the wide swath of bandage on her son's chest. "How're you feeling?"

"The nurse said I was a big fella." He held up his new toy and flipped open the hood. "She gave me a super-duper car."

Kristie shook her head when she saw that the woman was about to correct her son's assumption. "How would you like a ride in an ambulance?" she asked.

"With the siren blasting?" His bottom wiggled, but he kept his shoulder and arm perfectly still. "Is it gonna take us home?"

Bobby's mother brushed his light brown hair back and brushed a kiss across his forehead. "We're going to the hospital for a few days. The doctors say I can stay with you."

"Let's give them a couple of minutes alone, Doctor," Kristie whispered to Joshua, grinning up at him. To Bobby she said, "We'll be right back."

Joshua cupped her elbow and hustled her straight into their office. He kicked the door closed and pulled her into his arms. He needed to feel those capable hands of hers around him. He ended his self-imposed abstinence by kissing her, hard, as though the doubts he'd had, the doubts, that had kept him away from her, no longer mattered.

Though she was surprised by his brashness, her lips were parted, ready for the swift thrust of his tongue. With a tiny shudder, she surrendered to his kiss. Her hands splayed over his linen sports jacket, tracing up the hollow of his spine until she cradled his head in her hands.

"What was that for?" she gasped, when he finally came up for air. She buried her nose in the crook of his neck. He smelled of soap and after-shave—much better than rubbing alcohol and ointment.

He drew her hand from around his neck and placed kisses on the tips of her finger. "Me. My reward for being a big fella."

A sharp rap on the door—followed by Reid's head, poking through the crack he'd opened—had Kristie nimbly springing away from Joshua. Her fingers curled reflexively into her palm, as though she could hang on to the moment by pressing his kisses against the heartline in her palm.

"Bobby is being wheeled to the ambulance." Reid gave Joshua a hard glare. His unconcealed animosity contaminated Kristie's moment of bliss. "Sorry if I interrupted an important business discussion."

"Nothing we can't continue later," Joshua replied, struggling to appear composed when he badly wanted to shove Warner's face on the other side of the door and lock it.

Kristie harbored similar feelings. She could still taste Joshua's kiss when she flicked the tip of her tongue over her lower lip. She seldom resented duty's call, but this was the rare exception.

Turning to the small mirror hanging on the wall to check her appearance, she said, "I'll be right there, Reid."

For purely professional reasons, she was glad her smudgeproof lipstick lived up to the manufacturer's claims. She hastily restored her mussed hair by fluffing it with both hands as she strode toward the door.

"He's infatuated with you." Joshua, disliked the idea, and he speculated about whether there might be other, more valid reasons for Warner's possessiveness.

"Hardly." She paused in front of Joshua long enough to run her fingers along his jawline. "I've got to go say goodbye to Bobby."

Outside the office, Reid was waiting impatiently for her. "I've noticed how that Hayden guy looks at you."

"Oh?"

"Yeah. Like it was Christmas and you just fell off the top of the tree into his arms."

She tried to make light of the situation. "Me? A fallen angel?"

She turned to walk away, but he was hard on her heels. "What was going on in there? A little mouth-to-mouth resuscitation?"

"That's my business."

"Like hell."

His fingers bit into her upper arm. She stopped. Her blue eyes were icy as they traveled from his hand to his face. Her voice frosty, she said, "I beg your pardon, Dr. Warner?"

"When *I* flirted with you, you politely told me you weren't the ribbon on some package deal."

She peeled his fingers from her lab coat and continued on toward the waiting room. Only the fact that they worked well together kept her from telling him that his green eyes had had dollar signs stamped on their pupils. He'd shown more enthusiasm when he'd fondled the appointment book than in the faint attempt he'd made to hold her hand. She was convinced that all he'd ever wanted from her was a part-share in the clinics.

"Changed your mind, huh?" he muttered, catching up to her as she rounded the corner. "I guess I'd better quit flirting with you and giving my boss dirty looks or he'll terminate my contract.''

"Astute observation, Doctor," she told him as she neared Bobby's stretcher, which was being wheeled toward the entrance. She hoped any patients or employees who overheard her remark would assume they were discussing a professional matter. ''Why don't you enter that in your permanent records?''

Long after she'd waved at the ambulance and checked to make sure Bobby and his mother would be placed in a semiprivate room at the hospital, Kristie sat in the Cherokee next to Joshua, staring at his profile as he drove back to Ocala.

The Florida sunshine had bronzed the city pallor from his skin, she mused.

Mesmerized by the hint of a dimple in his cheek and her thoughts of their continuing the "discussion" Reid had interrupted, she hadn't heard a word he'd been saying.

"...the active files are computerized monthly. By June the new accounting programs will be written and the computers will be hooked up to a common terminal. The complaint file should shrink considerably by July."

Joshua paused when she didn't respond. A red light allowed him to glance at her.

"You aren't listening."

"No," she admitted, watching his other cheek for a twin indentation. It was smooth except for his five-o'clock shadow. The temptation to feel the rasp of them was too great to ignore. She reached over the stick shift and caressed his cheek. "You almost have a sexy dimple, right here."

The light turned green, but Joshua missed it. An impatient driver several cars back didn't; he hit his horn. Joshua goosed the gas petal. The engine roared; he'd forgotten to shift into second gear, because he'd been picturing the delicate wedge of dimples at the base of her spine.

"Almost?" He hiccuped, slightly embarrassed by his reaction to her touch.

Her fingers traced the weave of his white-on-white shirt, circling the edge of his cuff, playing along the ridges of his fingers until they dipped and climbed over the hills and valleys of his knuckles.

Her butterfly touch had him silently cursing the man who'd invented bucket seats. He'd have liked nothing better than to cuddle her under his arm. Her upswept hair left the shell-like curve of her ear vulnerable to similar sensuous exploration.

Kristie grinned as his hand tightened until his knuckles turned white. Her eyes drifted to the sprinkling of dark hairs on the backs of his hands. They sharply contrasted with the white French cuffs of his shirt. "You'd qualify as a WOLF 101 hunk."

He shifted gears, none too smoothly. "Is that some kind of medical jargon?"

"Uh-uh." She pointed to the radio, which was playing easy-listening music. "A couple of weeks ago a female deejay asked women to call in and describe what made a man eligible for a number one position in the man-watching charts."

"Dimples? That's what turns women on?"

"Actually, dimples come in fourth."

She leaned across the gap between the bucket seats. The muscles in his jaw quivered when she touched the tiny lines radiating from the corners of his eyes. His bi-

ceps bunched into a tight knot when the womanly fullness of her breast grazed his arm.

Joshua managed to keep the Cherokee below the
speed limit, but his own motor was racing wildly.

"Sylvester Stallone eyes . . . broad shoulders . . . great
buns . . . Very, very sexy."

He risked taking his eyes off the road. Did she realize what a turn-on it was for a man to hear a woman say
he was sexy?

"This is a hell of a time for this conversation," he
muttered. She blew lightly in his ear, and he shifted
deeper into the leather upholstery. "Did men get equal
radio time?"

"Mmm-hmmm." Her lips hummed against his earlobe. "But I missed hearing it."

Joshua made a sharp right turn. He muffled a groan
behind clenched teeth as the abrupt motion pressed her
more fully against his arm. He silently prayed that Cy-
press Lake Road led to a private spot!

"Why are we turning off the highway?"

"Because I can't concentrate on the road with your
sexy little body teasing me to distraction!"

The vehemence in his tone was sharply at odds with
the compliment. She shifted backward, plastering herself against the door. "Should I apologize for distracting you?"

"Only if you want to see a sexy WOLF weep!"

"What about Drew? Aren't you going to pick him up
from school?"

"Dusty offered to pick him up any time I'm late."

Sighting an unpaved road, Joshua made a left turn.
The road began to weave between century-old cy-
presses. He made another turn onto twin tracks of sand

with a growth of knee-high weeds that told him it was seldom traveled.

Kristie jiggled and bounced, clutching the sides of her seat, until Joshua made one more turn, into an abandoned orange grove. He slammed on the brakes, simultaneously twisting the key with one hand and releasing the seat level with the other. An instant later he circled her waist and dragged her into his lap.

The kiss they'd shared in her office was pure sweetness and light compared to the torrid passion he unleashed now. She surrendered willingly, curling up against him. She gloried in the feeling of his fingers luxuriating in the silkiness of her hair, tilting her head one way, then the other. He slanted his mouth to make delicious forays between her parted lips. The tiny groans she made were quickly swallowed by him.

"Want to know what's been driving me wild today, lady?" His breath feathered across her cheeks as his lips moved to the sensitive area beneath her ear. His hand moved down the curve of her collar to the shadowed vee of her breasts where he traced the scalloped lace of her bra through the tropical print of her blouse. "It's lime green."

Feigning astonishment, she whispered, "You peeked?"

"And speculated," he confessed, not an ounce of guilt in his voice. "There are advantages to my being taller than you. Lime green lace bikinis?"

She nodded, squirming in his lap. He groaned his appreciation of her honest reply.

"Yesterday. Sky blue?"

She had to think; it was difficult, what with him popping the buttons loose on her blouse. "Uh-uh. Peach. Blue the day before—" her nipple budded as he unclasped her bra and cupped her breast with his hand, ''... yesterday.''

''Sexy. Very, very sexy,'' he murmured, quoting her. He was getting hotter by the second. ''About as sexy as knowing that if I removed the comb from your hair it would cascade into my hands. Or listening to the whisper of silk on silk as you cross and uncross your legs.''

''I didn't think you were aware I was in the office with you.'' Pleased to know different, she covered his hands with hers and asked, ''Why haven't you been curious about the color of my nightgowns?''

''It wasn't lack of curiosity... or lack of imagination. I dream of you nightly, in every shade and hue between pristine white and slinky black.''

He worried her taut nipple with his thumb until she cradled his head so that he could lave it with his tongue.

''Then why, Joshua? Why haven't you come to me?''

''No invitation.''

Her gasp revealed her pleasure and her surprise. ''You pretend to ignore me at work and expect me to send you an engraved invitation to my bedroom?''

''Yes.'' He nuzzled her a little longer, then lifted his head. Their eyes met—hers a bewildered blue, his an earnest brown.

''I have to know you want me'' was the only explanation he offered for his contradictory behavior.

''I do.'' To prove it, she quickly shed her blouse and bra. She was in the process of unzipping her skirt when she realized he hadn't moved a muscle. ''Isn't the feeling mutual?''

''Now? In a car, in the middle of nowhere?''

Her hands framed his face. ''Anywhere, anytime, anyplace. I don't need monogrammed satin sheets and fluffy pillows. I need you.''

Joshua crushed her against him and held her so tightly that his fingers dug into her ribs.

She had no way of knowing the effect of what she'd said had on him. Somewhere in the dark recesses of his subconscious mind the wound of being told to get out of his wife's bed, that she didn't want him, had never wanted him, began to heal.

Eyes squeezed shut, he mumbled, "God, Kristine, knowing what I've told you, what Drew's said, I thought you'd decided to keep your distance. I would. You should find a man without a past, without mistakes or regrets."

"Maybe I should." His hold loosened. She took a deep breath and met his gaze directly. "You changed 'impossible' to 'I'm possible.' Can't you change your self-image from 'imperfect to I'm perfect?' Or at least change it to 'I'm perfect for Kristine?' Please?"

Her eyes silently begged him to love her, not for the sake of his job or for the clinics or for any other material reason, but for the sake of the growing love she felt for him. She couldn't change his past. She could only change his future. If he'd let her.

A slow smile tugged at the corner of his mouth. I'm perfect for Kristie, he silently repeated. It sounded so right, so true. I'm perfect for Kristie. The other corner raised until a genuine smile allowed a chuckle to rumble from deep in his chest.

His laughter infected her with his inner joy. "Is that a yes?"

For once his head and his heart weren't contradicting each other. His whole body was shaking when he pulled her back into his arms. His voice was a guttural hiss of emotion. "Yes."

Kristie's eyes sparkled with exhilaration. She reached over his shoulder, through the opening between the seats, and pulled down the back seat.

"Make love with me, Joshua," she said, clambering into the makeshift bed and shedding the remainder of her clothing. Her hand swung toward the open window. "Right here. Out in the middle of nowhere, with nothing but the scent of orange blossoms on the breeze, blue skies overhead . . . and me."

Her arms opened for him; her fingertips beckoned to him.

It was the invitation he'd been waiting for.

Later he would be amazed by his agility. It was a minor miracle for a man his size to undress without knocking his head on the ceiling or breaking the rearview mirror with his elbow or ripping the upholstery with his shoes. He did it, though. In fifteen seconds flat.

"Joshua, I love you," Kristie murmured, enfolding him in her arms, loving the feel of his weight pressing her into the carpet. She'd been thinking it; she'd had to say it. She placed her finger on his lips when he lifted his head. "Shh, you don't have to repeat it after me. I just want you to get used to the idea of being loved."

He gathered her solidly against him. She arched against his hardness, opening to him as naturally as the orange blossoms in the orchard welcomed the bees.

"Don't make me wait," he begged, impatient to be one with her.

"Come to me, Joshua. I'm filled with love for you."

The driving rhythm he initiated tightened the already-taut coil inside her. She clung to him, circling his waist with her legs, murmuring his name between short, panting breaths.

His culmination was dangerously close, and he captured her hips and held her still.

Kristie felt certain that the earth had stopped rotating on its axis. Her fingers dug into his shoulders when he withdrew from her. He couldn't leave her like this! She'd go crazy!

"Joshua?"

"Hush, little one." He raised her hips higher; his head lowered; her slender legs draped over his shoulders. He could have vaulted selfishly over the pinnacle of rapture with one hard thrust, but he wanted her passion fully released. "Let me love you, completely."

And he did, thoroughly, until her insides felt as though they'd melted and his tongue had sipped the very essence of her being bone-dry. Again and again he carried her to ecstatic heights.

When she thought there couldn't possibly be more, he lowered her, then surged masterfully inside her. Her muscles convulsed against him until they both felt waves of thrilling completion sweep them into oblivion.

She'd fainted. Or she'd hyperventilated. Or she'd died. She didn't know which it was, but if it was the last she knew there was definitely a heaven.

She sighed heavily, cuddling against Joshua's chest, and clung to her unbelievably happy state of mind.

Seven

It was Kristie who spotted the package sticking out of the mailbox at the end of the drive. "The mailman must've missed delivering it with the regular mail."

Joshua slowed the Cherokee to a stop. As she leaned through the window to reach inside the mailbox, he removed his appreciative dark eyes from her backside long enough to glance down the lane toward the house.

From this distance he could barely differentiate between Drew and his new friend. They both wore jeans and surfer T-shirts, and they were of similar height and build. Only Drew's dark hair made it possible for Joshua to tell who was handling the lead rope attached to the new filly's halter.

One of these years he'd get over his fear of arriving home and finding Drew gone.

"That's odd." Kristie sat back, her leg folded under her, and closed the door. "There are no postage stamps, and there's no return address." She passed the padded envelope to Joshua. "It's addressed to Drew."

He inspected the frail handwriting. He recognized it instantly. They'd gone back on their word. The Van Horns couldn't wait until August. Damn them and their false promises to let him make a life with Drew. He'd had a bellyful of their lies!

He pounded the steering wheel with his fist, then tossed the package on the back seat.

"Joshua?"

"I'd appreciate your not mentioning this to Drew. It's from his grandparents."

"No stamps and no return address. You think they're in the area, don't you, Joshua?"

"Yeah. They're here."

His jaw clenched into a hard knot. He glanced in the rearview mirror, half expecting a sleek silver Lincoln Town Car to be parked right behind him. No, they'd done their damage for today. They wanted him to sweat. His palms were damp as he shifted gears and drove the Cherokee down the lane.

"No strange car parked in front of the house," Kristie observed. With a note of optimism in her voice, she added, "Maybe they just left the package and went down the highway."

"There's something you have to understand about them, Kristine. What the Van Horns can't buy, they take. They've come for Drew."

"But that's illegal. You were granted custody by the courts! They can't—"

Joshua looked at her for a second, then brought his foot down harder on the accelerator. "Can and will."

"What are you going to do?"

"Exactly what I've been doing—keeping a close watch on Drew. When I registered him at school I left strict orders that he was not allowed to leave school property unless he was with me or Dusty. The only place they can get their hands on him is here. I hate to impose on your hospitality further, but I'm going to have to clue Maude and Dusty in on the problem. For the next few days I'll be working out of the office at the house. I'm not going to let Drew out of my sight."

"Are you going to tell Drew they're here?"

"No."

"Joshua, you can't build a fence around a kid his age without explanations. The first time you refuse to let him run over to Jenny's house or ride the back trail or go roaming on his own he'll rebel. He'll hate you more than he did the day you arrived here."

Joshua rolled to a stop beside the corral. He waved at Drew as though nothing out of the ordinary had happened, apart from his arriving home later than usual. "Be with you in a minute, son."

"You've got to talk to him." Kristie waved when both Jennifer and Drew made a comical face at her. "Today. Give him the package. Tell him you think his grandparents are planning to kidnap him."

"And watch him sneak out and hide in the bushes with his packed bags?" Joshua asked incredulously. "You've heard him say he prefers Boston, prefers living with them to living with me. I won't risk losing him again."

"Drew's whole attitude has changed. Look at him, Joshua! Ten days ago he would have spit in your eye rather than grin and make faces. You should give him a chance."

"Give him a chance to what? Let them get hold of him to poison his mind again? Money talks. They'll have him on a chartered plane headed for God knows where—Europe, South America, Australia—any place where it would take another prolonged court battle for me to get him back." Joshua shook his head vehemently. "Uh-uh. He's my son, damn it. His life is simple, uncomplicated. I'm going to make damn certain it stays that way."

"Let me give the package to Drew and talk to him. He'll listen to me."

"This isn't your problem, Kristine. It's mine. I'll take care of it."

Kristie kept him from opening the door by resting a restraining hand on his forearm. Her eyes begged him not to exclude her.

"I love you, Joshua, and I care about Drew, too. Do you honestly think I'm going to sit on my hands and whistle 'Dixie' while you shut me out of a difficult part of your life?"

He looked at her, his haunted eyes level with hers. He knew the Van Horns were ruthless when they wanted something as badly as they wanted Drew. If Kristie got in the way, they'd grind her beneath their elegant heels without breaking stride.

This conviction gave him the inner strength to protect her by softly saying, "I never came to you, Kristine. I don't need your help any more than your father did. Don't be a nuisance, or we'll have to leave, too." He knew how much he was hurting her, but it was for her own good.

He was out of the Cherokee and striding toward the two children before Kristie had recovered from the verbal slap. Her hands balled in her lap. A curtain of blond hair swung forward as she bent her head, determined not to cry.

She'd gambled her self-respect and her pride on the chance that he felt something for her. He'd taken both, along with a love he didn't want. She'd made a nuisance of herself.

It was all she could do to keep from folding her arms on the dashboard and bursting into tears.

"Kristie! Telephone!" Maude called from the kitchen door. "It's person-to-person, collect, from the Bahamas."

"Dad!" she whispered, hastily getting out of the vehicle and running into the house.

"Hurry up, child. This is the second time he's called. Must be important."

"I'll take it in the office." Her hand trembled as she picked up the receiver. "Dad?"

"Hi, sweetheart. How's it going?"

His voice sounded better—stronger and happier—than it had in months.

"Fine." Terrible! she added mentally. I told Joshua I loved him. He told me I'm a damn nuisance! "How's the fishing?"

"Great. How're the clinics doing? Am I going to recognize them when I get back?"

"Only if you hurry." She forced a brittle chuckle into the receiver. "Joshua's been busy."

"Doing a good job, huh? Have you two declared a truce?"

"He does his job. I do mine." She hoped the words weren't as bitter as they felt. She blinked and raised her eyes to the ceiling.

"Do I need to rush back?"

Selfishly she wanted her father to come home; self-lessly she wanted him to stay in the Bahamas until he regained all his old vigor.

"No. Everyone misses you, but we're holding down the fort until you get back."

"Good girl. I miss you, too. Is Joshua around?"

"He's in the corral with Drew. Do you want me to buzz the line out there?" For several seconds there was no response. "Dad?"

"I'm here. I can't discuss business with Joshua in the stable. Listen, sweetheart, I'm at Mike Pandolfo's condo. Why don't you have Joshua give me a call here later tonight?"

"Fine."

Carlton chuckled. "Where's your curiosity, child? Aren't you going to bug me to find out what I've got cooking down here?"

"Smelly fish, I imagine," she retorted. "You are sticking to your diet, aren't you?"

"I haven't had canned tuna once this week—just mouth-watering dishes of snapper, grouper and jew-fish. Mike's sister is a heavenly cook."

"Don't let Maude hear you compliment another cook. She's been force-feeding us dark green vegeta-bles because Joshua mentioned to her that Drew re-fused to eat them. This morning I had green flakes in my shredded wheat."

"Green flakes of what?"

"I was afraid to ask. She killed my curiosity last night when I saw her pouring green beans into the blender. We ate them. But I'm not sure how or where."

She heard Carlton laugh; then he placed his hand over the receiver and spoke to someone. Was that a fe-male voice she heard?

"I've got to run. It was good talking to you, Kristine. Tell Joshua to call me after ten. Okay?"

"Yeah. I'm glad you called, Dad."

"Don't work too hard. Bye."

She'd barely returned the phone to the hook when it rang.

"Fairbanks residence," she said automatically.

She could hear music playing, but no one spoke.

"Kristine Fairbanks speaking. Hello?"

Click. Kristie stared thoughtfully at the phone for a moment. Then, very gently, she returned it to its cradle.

A package with no return address. A phone call with no one on the other end of the line. It didn't take a genius to figure out who had called and who they wanted to speak to. She wondered if Drew's grandparents had tried to contact him before she and Joshua had returned from work.

She left the office and hurried down the corridor to the kitchen. The aroma of fried chicken and freshly baked biscuits enveloped her when she walked into the kitchen. Maude was humming off-key as she poured redeye gravy into a bowl.

"Maude, we haven't had any weird phone calls today, have we?"

"Weird?" Maude shrugged, then grinned. "No weirder than usual. An aluminum-siding salesman wanted to sell me his stuff. I had him explain how they'd make it stick to the brick and then I told him I only rented the house I live in."

"No one called and hung up?"

"A heavy breather?" She smacked the spoon against the side of the gravy bowl. "No such luck. Why?"

"Drew's grandparents dropped a package at the mailbox, for one thing. And when I answered the phone just now there was no one on the other end of the line."

Maude turned from the stove and carried the gravy to the table. "Why would Drew's grandparents do that? The boy would love to see or hear from them."

"Joshua wouldn't. He wants Drew to settle in here before he sees them."

"Tsk. Tsk. Tsk." Maude shook her head, then poked her wire-rimmed glasses higher on the bridge of her nose. "What's this old world comin' to when children can't see their grandfolks?"

"Joshua had to fight to get custody of Drew," Kristie explained. "He's afraid they'll try to kidnap Drew."

"Steal the boy? How can you steal something that's a part of you?" Maude nodded her head toward the barn. "Dusty and me weren't blessed with children of our own, but I'd feel real sorry for anybody who tried to stop me from seeing you, Kristie. Real sorry."

"But there's a big difference, Maude. You would never have tried to take me away from Carlton."

Maude wiped her hands on her apron and stared at Kristie. She pulled out a chair and sat down at the table.

"Kidnap you? No. But there was many a day I wished you were mine. Between your father's wishin' he was dead and his tryin' to work himself to death, he didn't have the time or the energy to show you how much he loved you." Maude grinned when she saw Kristie's reaction. "Close your mouth, child, or you'll be catchin' flies."

Stunned by Maude's confession, Kristie was unable to speak. She'd always known they cared for her, even loved her, but she'd had no idea how much. She sank down in the chair across from Maude.

She sandwiched Maude's hands between her own. Those hands had cooked her meals, washed her, paddled her bottom when she'd needed it and held her face close to her motherly bosom when she'd needed that, too. She loved Maude and Dusty.

"I've never really believed that Carlton loved me."

"He loved you, honey. It's hard for a man to raise a girl-child by himself." Her work-worn fingers curled around Kristie's thumb. "Joshua loves his boy. I just hope he's doin' right by him."

"I love Joshua, Maude." Kristie rubbed the back of Maude's hand with her cheek. "Why do I love people who can't love me in return?"

After several moments of painful silence, Maude sighed heavily and patted the side of Kristie's face. "There's no explaining love, child. Those that need love the most don't get it, and those that don't want love drown in it. Funny, though, I'd have guessed that Joshua needs all the love he can get, plus some."

"You're lucky to have Dusty."

Maude grinned, braced her arms on the table and got to her feet. "Yeah. Me and my Dusty Rhoades. Speakin' of Dusty, you'd better ring down to the barn for him while I pop dinner into the microwave."

"You will promise to keep an eye out on Drew, won't you?"

"I'm not likin' the idea of keeping a child away from his grandparents, but I'll do it," Maude promised. "Don't be thinkin' I won't tell Joshua what's on my mind, though."

* * *

"I hate dumb old homework," Drew muttered, flipping through the pages of his math book until he found a folded sheet of paper.

Kristie brought the latest *Journal of American Medicine* to the dining room table, where Drew was sitting, and began scanning the articles. Straight-faced, she muttered, "Me too, but it's better than being roped into doing the dishes."

"Yeah. Poor Dad. The night I helped Maude she lectured me on being a picky eater." Drew grinned. "Dad hid his peas under his mashed potatoes. Do you think she's scolding him about growin' up to be a ninety-eight-pound weakling?"

From the gleam she'd seen in Maude's eyes when she'd drafted Joshua to unload the dishwasher, Kristie felt certain that Joshua was getting his ear chewed, and not about hiding his green peas.

"I think you'd better get busy on your homework."

"Can I use the calculator?"

"Nope."

"How many times does nine go into seventy-two?"

"Six?"

"Six times nine is only fifty-four."

"Try seven, then." Kristie crooked her fingers over her mouth to keep from chuckling. "Maybe eight. How much is nine times nine?"

Drew frowned at her and slouched lower in his chair. "You're no help."

"I'll help—when you need it."

"Grown-ups," Drew muttered. "They sure can be dumb when they wanna be."

"Yep," Kristie agreed. "That's why we have kids— to keep us on our toes. How much is eight times nine?"

"Seventy-two." He was intent on getting Kristie to do the work for him and he didn't realize that his automatic response was the answer to his own question for a second or two. When it did, he winked at Kristie. "With a little practice you could have my homework done in no time."

"Believe me, Drew, it'll be much faster if you do it. Dusty used to make me write out the whole times table when I asked him for the answers."

"Oh." Drew heaved a monstrous sigh, straightened in his chair and picked up his pencil. "I don't suppose you wanna talk about the big secret Dad told me, do you?"

"Delaying tactics, Drew?"

Drew's dark eyes were lit with mischievousness. "You want me to tell it to you, don't you?"

"No. I imagine Joshua will tell me anything he wants me to know. Right now I want you to do your homework."

"It wasn't really a secret," he told her. "He said I could tell you. I sure hope I don't forget what it is before I finish my homework."

Cocking one eyebrow and shaking her head, Kristie turned to the next page of her journal.

"We're gonna move, soon!" Drew crowed happily. "We're gonna have our very own house and barn and everything!"

The words blurred in front of her eyes, but she didn't look up at Drew. She couldn't. Joshua had included her in his professional life, but he'd excluded her from his personal life.

She told Drew exactly what she'd prescribed for herself: "Get busy."

* * *

"Wait a minute, young lady," Maude said when she saw Kristie breeze through the kitchen, grab a piece of buttered toast from the table and head for the door. "You have plenty of time for breakfast. Besides, Joshua talked to Carlton and—"

"Later, Maude. Reid called in sick. I'll be at the Winter Park clinic."

Kristie was in her Mustang with the motor running when she heard the kitchen door slam and heard Joshua calling her name. She turned up the radio and backed the car out of the garage, determined to avoid him.

She almost had second thoughts when, nearing the end of the lane, she glanced in the rearview mirror and saw him chasing after her on foot, waving one arm high over his head.

"Too bad," she grunted, pulling onto the highway. "Whatever he and Dad cooked up together on the phone last night, they can damn well eat it themselves."

She'd made plans, too, small vital ones. But, she told herself, beginners take small, cautious steps, don't they? It was time she stood on her own two feet, independent of any man, be he father or lover.

Velma handed a new-patient form to Kristie and nodded toward the reception area. "She insists on seeing the person in charge of the clinic. Says she called all the clinics before she located you."

"If she wants the person in charge, you'd better see her," Kristie replied cheekily, handing the form back to the nurse.

"She wants to see a doctor—a *real* doctor." Velma affected a fake German accent. "Vell? Shall I put Mrs. Van Horn in ze room with ze fake diplomas?"

"Van Horn?" Kristie's eyes widened. "Does she have a Boston accent?"

"You must have overheard her griping about no place to *pahk* her *cah*."

Kristie took the form. The fragile writing matched that she'd seen on Drew's package. "I'll show Mrs. Van Horn back into my office, Velma. I don't think she's here for medical treatment."

Though the reception room was full of patients, Kristie had no trouble picking Mrs. Van Horn out of the crowd. She was the impeccably dressed woman who looked as though her daily supply of bottled water came directly from Ponce de Leon's fountain of youth.

"Mrs. Van Horn?" Kristie gave her a bright Florida smile that she hoped would send the woman running from the clinic in search of her suntan lotion. "I'm Dr. Fairbanks."

The older woman regally presented her gloved hand. "I'm Drew's grandmother, Juliet Van Horn. I'd like a word with you in private."

The catch in the older woman's voice and the momentary flash of discomfort in her eyes when Kristie lightly squeezed her fingertips made Kristie discard her preconceived notions and look beneath her outward appearance.

"Arthritis?"

"Yes. Chronic."

That explains the gloves, Kristie thought as she watched Mrs. Van Horn slowly rise. To a less practiced eye her movements might have appeared effortless; to Kristie they indicated painful swelling of the joints.

Kristie led the way to her office. "Can I get you anything? Coffee? Tea?"

"My grandson," Mrs. Van Horn replied succinctly.

Kristie sat down behind the desk. "You don't mince words, do you?"

"No." She opened her purse, withdrew a sealed envelope and placed it on the desk. "Take this check and bring the boy to me at the Peabody Hotel."

It wasn't a request; it was a demand. The empathy Kristie had felt for the woman because of her arthritis waned. She wanted to rip the envelope in two and toss it in her wrinkle-free face.

"I don't need your money, Mrs. Van Horn."

The older woman arched her brow; which Kristie felt certain she would never have done if she'd known how many wrinkles the gesture could cost her.

"Name your price. If not money, what?"

"I can't help you."

Mrs. Van Horn's shoulders sagged. "I only want to see Drew. Hold him. When he left Boston he was so . . . so angry."

Kristie leaned forward, feeling compelled to comfort her. "Drew isn't angry with you, Mrs. Van Horn."

"He should be." Her hand shook visibly as she removed one glove, opened her purse and pulled out a linen handkerchief. She dabbed at the corners of her eyes. "My husband and I were so caught up in battling for permanent custody, we lost sight of what we were doing to Drew. We didn't realize that twisting the truth and alienating the child from Joshua could hurt Drew, too. If you could bring him to me for just a few minutes, long enough for me to tell him the truth, then I'll go back to Boston and wait for his summer visit."

"I can't." The thought of sneaking around behind Joshua's back was enough to send shivers up her spine. "Let me talk to Joshua. Maybe I can convince him—"

"No! No one could could convince Joshua to believe anything good about me. You don't understand." Her proud head dropped to her chest. Shame softened her voice until Kristie could barely hear her. "I did everything I could do to blacken Joshua's name in front of the judge. I took half-truths and twisted them until...until...they were lies. Drew believed them. I can't blame Joshua for believing I'll poison Drew's mind against him. But I won't. I promise."

Kristie's heart went out to the woman. She wanted to tell her that Joshua didn't hate the Van Horns, but she couldn't speak for him. Despite the youthful appearance that Mrs. Van Horn's wealth had bought her, Kristie pitied her.

But she couldn't let pity spoil Joshua's and Drew's chance for happiness. Mrs. Van Horn admitted having lied in court. She might be twisting the truth right now. Only the sincerity in her voice made her believable.

"My hands are tied, Mrs. Van Horn. I can't bring Drew to you, and I can't blame Joshua for not trusting you."

"Five minutes. Put the flag up on your mailbox when Joshua isn't there and give me five minutes alone with Drew. Is that too much to ask? I swear, I won't do anything to upset Drew. I only want to hold him and tell him the truth. I love him, Dr. Fairbanks."

"This could be a trick," Kristie said. "You could kidnap Drew. He wouldn't be the first child abducted by a close relative."

"I won't lie to you." Her tear-dampened eyes met Kristine's direct stare. "I've thought about it. But neither my husband nor I is physically able to traipse around the world hiding Drew."

"What if Drew asks you to take him back to Boston with you? What would you do?"

Kristie didn't believe Drew would make that decision, but she knew teenagers were unpredictable. Joshua was a firm disciplinarian; the Van Horns might not be. Any teenager would be tempted to live where he could call the shots.

"I give you my word." She laid her gnarled hand across Kristie's slender hand. "Five minutes. That's all I'll take."

Touched by Mrs. Van Horn's strong emotional appeal, swayed by what Maude had said about grandparents' rights, but knowing that Joshua would consider her interference a betrayal, Kristie was caught in a dilemma.

"Think about it," Mrs. Van Horn said, patting Kristie's hand, then rising slowly. "I'll know your decision when I see the red flag raised on your mailbox."

Eight

You're late," Joshua observed simply.

Kristie crossed the threshold of her bedroom, uncertain of his reason for being there. He'd never come to her. Wasn't that what he'd said, right before he'd called her a nuisance? Did he know about Mrs. Van Horn's visit? Did he know that in her emotional turmoil Mrs. Van Horn had forgotten to pick up the envelope she'd left on the desk, and that Kristie had tucked it in her purse for safekeeping? Guiltily Kristie clutched the purse to her chest.

Joshua was stretched out on the ivory satin coverlet, his hands folded behind his head; his relaxed posture would probably have fooled someone who didn't know what a man of contradictions he was.

"The clinic was packed. I had paperwork to catch up on." She dropped her purse on the dresser and instantly regretted it. Her empty hands felt awkward. "I didn't expect you to be waiting for me," she said hastily.

"Didn't you?" His voice was cool, but Kristie could hear anger bubbling beneath the surface. "Did you think I'd chase after your car like a dog and not be waiting by your hearth when you returned?"

"I expect the unexpected from you." Her right hand moved toward the lamp on the dresser.

"Leave it off."

She turned the switch. "I prefer to conduct our discussion with as much illumination as possible."

"Ah, yes. Illumination." He turned onto his side and flicked on the bedside lamp. "Come here, Kristie. I'd like you to shed some light on why you didn't return my calls today."

Something inside Kristie warned her that Joshua needed careful handling in his present mood. She hadn't done anything wrong—at least not yet. The red flag on the mailbox was still horizontal. She'd contacted Doug, the company's attorney, to have her company stock put in Carlton's name again, but that was none of Joshua's business.

With determined nonchalance, she kicked off her black patent-leather heels and removed her checkered jacket. The earrings were next. She tried to toss them into the jewelry box and missed.

"Were they important?" she asked, her voice husky with nervousness. He patted the side of the bed while she blindly hunted for the gold hoops.

"The first one was. I wanted to chew your butt for racing out of here before I could discuss Carlton's latest business venture with you."

"Oh." Locating one earring and getting it into the velvety-lined box was the only constructive thing she could think of to do with her hands. Her fingers feathered frantically over the polished mahogany surface. "I spoke to Carlton last night. If he'd wanted me informed, he'd have told me about it himself." And if you'd wanted to inform me about your leaving here you should have, she added silently. She was heartily tired of never being consulted!

"No, Kristie. We both know damn well that he hired me to be the bearer of all tidings—good and bad."

To hell with the earrings, she thought. How intimidating could a fully clothed man lying flat on his back be? Unless he had X-ray vision, he didn't know that Juliet Van Horn's envelope was in her purse. She'd take the initiative and give him something to be steamed about.

She straightened her shoulders and said, "I had my corporate shares transferred back to Carlton."

"Call number two. Doug must have called Carlton. Carlton called me to find out what was going on. I wish I knew what was going on in your mind."

She narrowed the space between them, swaying her hips provocatively in the process. "Why? Isn't it *convenient* for me to be practically penniless?"

"Low blow, Kristie," he growled. "Come closer. See if you hit your mark. Did you stop to think that *if* I were interested in your money—which I'm not—I could marry you and bide my time until Carlton died and you inherited those stocks?"

She hadn't thought that far into the future, but she wasn't about to admit that to Joshua.

"What is this, Joshua? An inquisition?"

His long legs swung to the edge of the bed. Quicker than a Florida panther he was off the bed, imprisoning her arms in his hands. "Did you sign over those damn stocks because of me? Do you think I give a damn if you own half the clinics?''

She'd struck a nerve. The muscle along his jawline flexed. She tilted her head back until her blue eyes blazed into his. ''When you eavesdropped on a private conversation between me and Carlton you heard him say he wouldn't object to my marrying you. Do you remember what I said?''

''You'd only marry for love.''

''And when we made love you told me you'd married once for convenience. Why not marry again, for the same reason?''

''Because a man can get lost and end up in hell, but he doesn't willingly choose to make it his permanent address. That's why.'' His eyes burned with anger and indignation. He stared at her for a long moment, then took a deep breath. ''But that isn't the only reason you dumped your stock back in Carlton's lap, is it?''

''No, not entirely.''

''Call number three. Why?''

''You wouldn't understand.''

''Try me.'' His fingers soothed the places they'd clutched so savagely a moment before. ''Why, Kristie?''

''It was something Maude said. Or maybe she didn't say it, but it was a feeling I had after I'd talked to her.''

Kristie twisted out of his light grip and went over to the window. She parted the drapes. She needed to look at the starry sky to combat this feeling of being sealed in an empty vacuum.

''You know the trite saying, about not being able to buy love? Maude tried to teach me that, but I had to learn it when I was Drew's age—the hard way.'' She fixed her eyes on the North Star, hoping that what she was about to tell Joshua would guide him to a closer understanding of her. "I walked Maude's legs down to the anklebone one year shopping for a Christmas present for Carlton with the dimes and nickels I'd saved from my lunch money. Oh, I know. Carlton would have given me the money to shop for him, but I thought if it was my money, if I could find something superspecial, he would have to love me, wouldn't he?"

Kristie shook her head sadly in reply to her own rhetorical question. "I found a crystal star that looked like it had fallen from heaven just for me to give to Carlton. I must have asked Maude and Dusty a million times if I'd bought the right gift. I'd wrap it and put it under the tree, then sneak back down, unwrap it and make wishes on it. I must have used a dozen rolls of paper. And then Christmas morning came. Maude gave him a robe. Dusty gave him a belt buckle. I gave him a wishing star."

Kristie glanced over her shoulder. Joshua was so still that for a moment she'd thought she was alone.

"Do you know what Carlton said? The same thing he said to Dusty and Maude—'That's real nice.'" A sound that might have been a laugh passed through her lips. "Real nice, huh? I couldn't buy his love, not even with a star, so I tried to earn it. I tried to do everything he'd done, only I tried to do it better. Another piece of folly on my part. Last night, though, when I talked to Maude, I realized how much she loved me. I thought about that all night. I didn't buy it or earn it…she gave it freely. No strings. No charge. No guarantees."

"And you decided to set Carlton free by giving the stock back to him?"

"Yeah. The clinics were one more attempt on my part to hold on to him. He can have them with my blessings."

A muscle moved convulsively in Joshua's throat as he swallowed the constriction there. The truly pitiful part was that Carlton wouldn't understand her grand gesture. He'd think it was some attempt on her part to get him back to Florida.

He had to tell her about the business deal Carlton had proposed. Sooner or later she'd find out, and when she did she'd have more reasons to doubt him. He didn't want to be held responsible for hurting her.

"Kristie, this is one hell of a bad time to tell you this, but Carlton wants to open a free clinic in the Bahamas. He plans on practicing medicine on a part-time basis." Joshua's eyes dropped to his toes as he said, "He wants to sell me his share of the Florida clinics."

The irony of the situation made Kristie grin. In signing over the stock she'd thought she was making a definite statement that Carlton would understand clearly. She'd only wanted to be a part of the clinics because they were the biggest part of his life. Now it appeared that her father didn't care about her or the clinics.

"Looks as though neither of the Fairbankses will be in the doc-in-the-box business much longer."

"Call five." He tilted her chin up with one curved finger. "Your father intends for us to be partners."

"No, Joshua. I won't reconsider keeping the stocks."

His mouth slanted, lowering closer to hers. "I don't give a damn whether or not we're business partners. I nearly went crazy when I couldn't reach you today. When you didn't come home I thought I'd be physically ill."

"Joshua..." She had to tell him about Mrs. Van Horn's visit. About the check. About the mailbox. "Don't..."

"I love you, Kristine." He folded her into his arms and held her as though she were infinitely precious to him. "I swore I'd never let another woman make me weak, vulnerable. No woman would ever complicate my life again. It was just going to be Drew and me against the world. Only it didn't work out that way. I love you."

"Stop. Please." She twisted in his arms but he held her close. "I have to tell you who came by the clinic."

"Shush, love." His lips brushed across hers in a light caress. "There's only one thing I want to hear from those sweet lips of yours. Tell me I haven't let my past ruin our future. Give me your love—freely. I can't buy it or earn it. You have to give it to me. No charge. No strings. No guarantees. That's how I love you."

She hated the thought of spoiling this precious moment, but she had no choice. As his lips moved across her face, she whispered, "Juliet Van Horn came to see me."

"To hell with her," he growled, following the curve of her lip with his tongue.

"But, Joshua, she only wants to be able to hold her grandson in her arms for five minutes."

"No."

"She thinks you hate her."

"I do—and with good reason."

He kissed her into a momentary silence. Joshua loved her. That was all that mattered, wasn't it? She wanted to wrap herself around him and let the world take a flying leap. Her head spun as he lifted her in his arms and carried her to the bed.

A slender thread of sanity made her say, "We have to talk about this, Joshua." She couldn't let him put her in one compartment of his life, with Drew and his grandparents in another niche.

"The hell we do. Closed file, Kristie." When she shook her head, he framed her face with his hands. "I'm not going to let her lies spoil our love."

"She admitted that she'd lied."

"She'll say anything to get what she wants. She wants Drew. She'll use you to get to him if you let her. I can't let that happen, Kristie. I'll do everything in my power to keep you and Drew safe from her."

She felt safe here in his arms. She circled his neck with her arms and melted against him. "Stay with me, Joshua. We'll keep each other safe."

On tiptoe, to avoid awakening his father, Drew scurried down the hallway toward Kristie's room. She'd come home too late for him to show her the A he'd gotten on his math paper or for him to make plans to go riding with her. But it was Saturday morning. Dusty said she was always up before dawn on Saturdays. That way she could ride before it got too hot.

He saw a sliver of light under the door. He rapped with his knuckles. "Kristie?" Then a little louder: "Kristie? Are you awake?"

Joshua's eyes popped open the moment he heard his son's voice. Kristie was sleeping soundly, snuggled against him spoon-fashion. He shook her shoulder as he tossed back the covers. Stark naked, he glanced around frantically for his clothing.

"Kristie? Are you decent?" Drew called.

Panicking at the thought of his son finding him here, Joshua shook Kristie again, harder this time, then scooped up their tangled clothing and darted into her bathroom.

"I'm gonna count to five, sleepyhead," Drew continued. "Then I'm gonna get some water and pour it over your head! That's what Maude said she used to have to do. *One!*"

Kristie sat bolt upright. The sheet dropped to her waist. Her eyes darted around the room, finally focusing on the unlocked door. "Drew?"

"Two!"

"I'm not dressed." She leaped from the bed and ran to the closet for her robe. "Don't you dare come in here!"

"Three!" Drew giggled. "*Four!* I've got a bucket of ice water out here."

Kristie shoved her arms in the sleeves of the robe, tied the belt haphazardly at her waist and made a mad dash for the door.

"Five!"

She turned the lock just as the knob twisted.

"You're no fun, Kristie."

No fun? The thought of Drew barging in and finding Joshua frantically yanking his jeans over his hips in her bathroom was enough to bring a hysterical giggle through the fingers she had clamped over her mouth.

Thinking quickly, she called, "Why don't you go fix yourself a bowl of cereal while I get dressed?"

"I'm not hungry."

"Okay. Go fix me a bowl of cereal. I'm hungry."

"Dad's still asleep. Do you want me to see if he wants to go riding with us?"

"No!" Her mind was racing as she tried to get one step ahead of Drew. "By the time we eat and saddle up the horses he'll be awake."

"What if he isn't?"

Kristie shook her head. She would gladly have given a king's ransom for a cup of coffee before having to answer Drew's questions. She had to think of something that would make damn certain Drew didn't run down to his father's room.

"Can we throw ice water on him?" Drew asked.

"Yeah!" Kristie agreed hastily. "That's it! We'll throw water on him."

The dirty look Joshua shot her could have been directed at the enthusiasm of her reply—or it could have been caused by his zipper getting caught on his underwear.

"You promise you won't let him ground me for the rest of my life?"

"I promise. Now scat, brat, so I can get dressed in peace."

She pressed her ear to the door to make sure he was gone, then burst into a fit of giggles.

"What's so damn funny?" Joshua whispered loudly.

"You."

"Me?"

"Yeah. You should have seen yourself hopping from one foot to the other and yanking on your zipper."

Now that there was no longer any immediate danger of his being discovered, his sense of humor was slowing being restored. Soon his smile was as wide as hers. "Turn around and look in the mirror, lady. It's a good thing you got the door locked in time. Otherwise I wouldn't have to explain anything about the birds and the bees to my son!"

Kristie whirled around. In her haste she'd adequately covered the upper half of her body, but the hem on one side of her robe was caught underneath the belt. Her face turned beet red. She corrected her oversight.

"I must've snagged a tooth in the zipper. They don't make jeans the way they used to," he complained as he pulled his shirt on. He left his shirttail out. "Get a move on, will you?"

"One burst of energy before coffee is my limit." Kristie picked up one of his socks and sidled lazily into the bathroom, where Joshua was diligently rummaging through the bundle of clothing he'd picked up earlier. His hands lingered longer than necessary on her lacy lingerie. She leaned against the doorframe, dangled the sock between her thumb and forefinger, close to his head, and quipped, "Want to trade? Lavender isn't your color."

He jackknifed up and grabbed for the sock; she put her arm behind her back.

"It's not nice to tease a man in the morning." He flattened his body against hers and fumbled for the sock, deliberately keeping his hand on her backside. His head dipped to her throat, and he nipped a path to her ear. Her fingers clenched tighter on the sock. "Give it to me."

The rasp of his dark whiskers along her throat made her tingle with anticipation. Her head lolled to one side, inviting further exploration. She wanted to give him one heck of a lot more than a dirty sock!

Distracted by the feel of her breasts budding against him, he whispered, "Did I tell you how beautiful you look with your hair mussed and your lips swollen from my kisses?"

She arched her hips against him; her fingers dived for the short hairs at his nape. "Uh-uh."

"Or how there's still a trace of your perfume right here?" His tongue laved an erotic circle at the pulse point in her throat. His knee parted her legs, and he rocked her against the hardness of his thigh. "Or how the thought of one tug on your belt being the only thing between me and the heavenly delights of your body is enough to drive me insane?"

"Uh-uh. You forgot to mention that, too."

He tongued her ear; she groaned.

"And how your cornflakes are getting soggy?" One yank and the sock was in his hand and he was striding across the room to find his shoes.

Stunned by his sudden disappearance, Kristie sagged against the wall momentarily. "That was an ornery trick, Joshua Hayden. I'll get you for that."

Chuckling, he scooped up his loafers and crossed to the door. Unlocking and opening it, he peeked down the hallway, found it empty and said over his shoulder, "I'll look forward to it. Hurry!"

Smoothing her hands over her tingling breasts, waist and hips, Kristie groaned in frustration. Fond though she was of Drew, she wasn't the least bit eager to rush to the breakfast table. Joshua had whetted her appetite for something far more exotic than dried cereal.

"Scoundrel," Kristie murmured, thinking of how he had tormented her. Delightfully wicked plans of how she'd get even began forming in her mind. She sashayed to the mirror, winked at her reflection and said, "He's gonna suffer—badly!"

The instant Kristie strode into the kitchen dressed in skintight jeans and a red crop top Joshua suspected he was in trouble. When she refilled his coffee cup and the side of her unrestrained breast accidentally-on-purpose brushed against his shoulder he knew he was in *deep* trouble!

"Dusty taught me how to rope a post," Drew boasted, totally unaware of what was going on between his father and Kristie. "He says you used to throw a mean lasso, too, Kristie. Can you really do rope tricks?"

Plucking a plump strawberry off the top of her cereal, she swirled the tip of her tongue around it, licked off its sugary coating, then slowly sank her teeth into the sweet berry. Juice spurted from the corner of her mouth. She licked it up.

Her eyes sparkled with mischief when she caught sight of Joshua's knuckles. They were turning white as his fingers tightened on his spoon.

"I've been known to do a couple of tricks," she answered, grinning, "Nothing fancy, though."

"Good thing you got up right after I did, Dad," Drew said, chortling. "We were gonna pull a different kind of trick on you. Ice water! Splash! Right in the center of your belly button!"

"I'll remember that one the next time I can't get you out of bed to go to school," Joshua told him good-naturedly. "What goes around comes around."

"What's that mean?"

Kristie smirked. "It means if you pull a dirty trick on somebody, you'll get one pulled on you."

Shivering, Drew said, "I'd better sleep on my stomach. Or I could lock my door, like you do."

The sound of boots scraping on the concrete outside the door caught their attention. Dusty strode inside, removed his battered hat and wiped his brow on his sleeve. "The farrier's here."

"On Saturday?" Kristie asked, puzzled.

"Says he and his missus are going to be gone for a couple of weeks. He wants to know if you want the hooves trimmed today or do you want to wait till he gets back."

Kristie glanced at Drew. "We'd planned on riding them this morning."

"Lazy Bones has a shoe loose," Dusty said. "If nothing else, the farrier has to replace it. 'Sides, it's already hotter than sin out there. I'd ride later this evening, when it cools down, if I was you folks."

Kristie knew that Drew had been looking forward to a long ride. "Why don't you call Jenny Lynn and invite her over for a swim in the pool?" she said to him. "We'll grill hot dogs for dinner, and then all four of us can go for a ride when it cools off."

At the mention of his friend's name, Drew's face brightened. He pushed his chair back. "She kinda hinted that she'd like to go swimming but they don't have a pool. Can I call her now?"

Kristie looked at Joshua.

"Go ahead, son."

While Kristie was watching Drew leave the kitchen, Dusty filched a berry from her bowl and popped it in his mouth. "I'll tell the farrier to go ahead."

Kristie glanced from the bulge in Dusty's cheek to her bowl, then back to the picture of innocence standing beside her. "You do that."

Recklessly Dusty reached for another strawberry. Kristie had her spoon ready. He snatched; she rapped.

"Gotcha!"

Dusty shook his fingers, shoved his hat back on his head and sauntered to the door. "No more berries out of my strawberry patch for you, stinkpot. Nary a one.

You better enjoy those, 'cause you ain't a-gonna get any more.''

"Dusty..."

He wheeled around, his hands cupped, and Kristie tossed him the biggest, ripest berry in her bowl. Dusty caught it and popped it in his mouth. Then he tipped his hat and swaggered out of the kitchen.

"Nothing pleases Dusty more than winning one of our little skirmishes."

"I'd have to put my money on you." He tilted his chair back. His eyes roamed appreciatively over her crop top. "No bra?"

"You noticed?" she asked, feigning amazement. "From the way your eyes have been glued to your bowl I thought you could read cornflakes like tea leaves."

"Oh, I *noticed*. I'd have done a lot more than sneak a peak if certain young eyes hadn't been watching."

"Promises, promises." Kristie felt safe in the knowledge that Drew would be back any minute. She picked up a strawberry and twirled it by its stem. "Talk, talk, talk. All wind and no rain."

Quick as a flash, the front legs of Joshua's chair hit the floor. He clamped his fingers on her wrist and tugged, bringing the strawberry to his lips. Greedily he sucked the berry—and her fingertips—into his mouth.

The hot juices of his mouth had the same effect on her fingers that a bobby pin stick in an electrical outlet would have. They sizzled. When he let go, she plopped none too gracefully back in her seat.

She only had time to say "Sexpot!" before Drew came back into the kitchen.

"Jenny's got a flat tire on her bike and doesn't want to walk all the way over here by herself. Do you care if I ride mine over there and we walk back together?"

Kristie shook her head to keep Joshua from giving his permission. The Van Horns were watching the mailbox for a signal. She didn't want Drew anywhere near it. "Why don't you and your dad take the car to get her while I straighten up the kitchen?"

"I could ride her on my handlebars."

"Uh-uh. I think Kristie has the best idea." Joshua stood up and placed his hands on his son's shoulders. "Tell you what—you go get the keys from the bedroom and start the Cherokee. I'll be right out."

"You mean it? I get to start the car?"

"Hurry up before I change my mind."

"I'll honk twice."

When she was certain Drew was out of hearing range, Kristie said, "Drew's grandmother told me to raise the flag on the mailbox if you agreed to let her see Drew."

"You should have told her to stay away from here," Joshua grunted, none too pleased with the idea of the Van Horns so close.

"What can I say? I felt sorry for her."

"Don't. She'll take advantage of your soft heart."

"I wish you'd reconsider, Joshua." She tilted her head back until she could see his face. "It's only five minutes."

"No. And that's final." He bent at the waist and kissed the tip of her nose to take the sharp edge off his refusal. "I'll be back in a few minutes."

There was a tinge of sadness in her blue eyes as she watched him walk away. She understood his reasons for not allowing unscheduled visitation rights, but— Oh, what the heck! She wasn't going to allow the Van Horns to be a grey cloud on a perfectly sunny day.

She jumped to her feet and rushed after him. "Joshua...I love you. Don't worry about me raising the mailbox flag. I'd never betray your wishes regarding Drew."

"Believe me, honey, I'm doing what's best for all of us." He had wondered if she would succumb to the Van Horns' persuasions. The way she cared for people, her softheartedness and sensitivity were the very things that had broken through the brittle shell he'd put around his heart. But her virtues could well lead to his downfall. He hugged her swiftly. "Don't let them get to you, love. On this one I'm right."

The horn blasted twice.

Aware that he also didn't want Drew to know about their relationship, she stepped away from him.

He slipped out the door, shouting, "Hold your horses! I'm coming!"

Kristie crossed to the table and began carrying the dishes to the sink. She wondered how long Joshua was planning on keeping what they felt for each other a secret from Drew. Joshua's son liked her, she knew. That should help, she mused, rinsing a clump of cereal from the rim of the bowl. She was the one Drew had pointed at and said, "You I'm gonna like." He'd hated most of the rest of the world, but he'd liked her.

And now that he'd stopped being surly and unreasonable, Kristie liked him, too.

"Mom," she muttered, trying the word on for size. "Stepmom?" She shook her head. The sound of it made her think of wicked witches, stepsisters and poisoned apples. "Kristie."

She squirted liquid detergent in the sink. There were only a handful of dishes. No point in running the dishwasher.

The idea of Drew being her son by marriage pleased her. Horseback riding and rope tricks weren't the only things she could teach him. Her elbows deep in the thick suds, she grinned at the prospect. Drew would grow up to be a son Joshua could be proud of. And maybe, just maybe, if they were lucky, he'd have a brother or sister. Being an only child, she liked that idea, too.

Nine

___

Don't do it!'' Joshua sputtered, treading water and fending Drew off.

"Do it, Kristie. Get him!'' Drew squealed. "Cannonball him!''

Joshua chuckled and shoved Drew aside. Jenny Lynn giggled and pulled on his arm. "She's no bigger than a bottle rocket. She'll fizzle before she hits the water.''

"I'll show you fizzle, mister.'' She took a running leap, tucked her legs under her seat and wrapped her arms around her knees. She landed within inches of Joshua's head.

"Tidal wave! Get him!'' Drew shouted. "Sink him!''

Kristie held her breath and swam around Joshua's churning legs. Before he could locate her, she wrapped her arms around his knees, then blew the air from her lungs. She was like a hundred-and-ten-pound rock tied to his legs.

When her air supply was totally depleted, she pushed away from him and swam to the shallow end of the pool. "Call me a bottle rocket, will you?" she yelled, gasping for breath.

A beguiling grin twitched the corners of Joshua's mouth when his head surfaced.

"Uh-oh!" The desire for revenge gleamed in his black eyes. "Drew! Jenny!"

"Your partners in crime have deserted you."

Kristie ducked her head to get the hair from her eyes. Both arms stuck out in front of her, she tried to fend him away.

"Say..." He paused, trying to think of something outrageous to make her say other than the trite 'uncle.' "Dusty snacks on alligators! Say it, or you're gonna be monster bait." Arms lifted, fingers splayed, he did an admirable impersonation of the star of *The Creature from the Black Lagoon.* "Say it."

"Never!"

He lowered his voice to a growl. "Say... never tease a 101 WOLF!"

"The kids are watching..." Kristie backed away until the wall of the pool touched her shoulders.

Joshua's eyes were plastered to her hibiscus-print bathing suit, which barely covered the subject it had been intended to conceal. "Just wait till I get you alone, lady," he said threateningly.

"Dad," Drew shouted from the other end of the pool, "we're gonna go over to the barn!"

The kids were out of the pool, wrapped in towels, their shoes in their hands, and running toward the barn before Joshua could shout, "Put your shoes on!"

Joshua watched them out of sight, then turned back to Kristie with a comic leer. Before she could think of a protest, he had circled her tiny waist with his hands and pulled her high against his chest.

"I could pitch you down there with one hand." Beneath the surface, his hand skimmed over the French-cut bathing suit until it touched the bare curve of her fanny. "I have to keep reminding myself how fragile you are."

"Just one short-people joke and I'll punch you so hard you'll have to grow gills to survive on the bottom of the pool."

"Such big threats from a little tyke."

"Ever heard of David and Goliath?"

"Yeah. Remind me to keep you away from sling-shots and rock piles."

The fingers feathering up her thighs were making thinking tough, damn tough. She wanted to kiss him. Lordy, Lordy, she wanted more than kisses. Clearing her throat to quench her sudden thirst for him, she added firmly, "We're even, Joshua."

"Even? Lady, I plan to get a head start on the next skirmish. You've been prancing around here, tantalizing me, for hours. The men in the white coats should arrive any minute!"

"They'd better bring two jackets," Kristie groaned. "Maybe we can be cellmates? Think of it. You and me confined in a ten-by-ten cell. Sounds heavenly."

"With my arms strapped around my middle? That's my idea of hell!"

"We'll think of something innovative," she promised. She raised her eyebrows and gave him a cheeky grin when she saw him glance toward her bedroom. "See? We aren't even locked up and your wheels are turning."

He lowered her legs until her feet touched bottom. "Actually, I'm wondering how long I'm going to have to stay in the water to keep from embarrassing myself." His gaze fell to his swim trunks. "There's no hiding room down there."

Kristie held her slightly shriveled hands in front of him. "Maybe..."

"Uh-oh. It doesn't." He edged backward. "Why don't you go light the grill? I'll check on the kids in a minute or two. Jenny's parents are going to pick her up around three."

"I guess Drew's a little old for us to insist on him taking a nap after company leaves, huh?"

"Unfortunately, yes."

"Ah, the joys of parenthood," she said sardonically as she sliced through the shallow water to the steps.

Guess that's the price adults pay for the fun of making babies, she mused.

She took a beach towel from the chaise lounge, bent at the waist and fluffed her hair. It wasn't as if she'd been consciously holding her breath waiting for Mr. Right to appear. But now that he was here she wanted him to run to the nearest church before the alarm on her biological clock started to ring. Silently she wondered how long Joshua was planning to keep Drew in the dark. Anything beyond the immediate future would test the limits of her patience.

"Be patient, Kristie," Joshua said as he pulled the girth strap on Misty Blue's saddle.

To have a minute alone with Kristie he'd offered to saddle up the horses while Drew finished playing a computer game. Dusty and Maude had gone to the grocery to stock up on supplies for the coming week.

"Drew's given you chances to tell him. He was the one who was telling Jenny about buying a house and it needing a woman's touch. It was the perfect opportunity for you to say something subtle."

"Like?"

Kristie grinned. She walked her fingers up the center of his back. Her forefinger landed square in his dimple when he looked over his shoulder. "You could have volunteered me as sort of a live-in decorator."

"Decorators don't live with their clients. Drew is naive, but he isn't stupid."

"You don't think he's noticed there's something going on between the two of us?"

"Nope. First of all, he thinks we're ancient, too old to play what he calls licky-face. And, secondly, when Jenny Lynn's around he doesn't notice anything. He's definitely been bitten by the lovebug."

"Then he won't mind sharing you with me." Cozying up next to Joshua, she playfully sank her teeth into his arm. "Now you've been bitten, too."

"Temptress." He snuggled her against his long, hard frame. Their mutual game of who-can-touch-whom-without-getting-caught had worn his back molars down to nubbins. He wanted to keep Drew's life simple until his son adjusted to living with him, but living in a state of perpetual arousal was enough to make a grown man weep. Joshua glanced toward the open barn doors and wondered aloud, "How long do you think it'll take Drew to finish his game?"

"At least fifteen minutes. You'll probably have to go back in and drag him out. Those games are addictive."

Joshua curled his arm around her waist and backed her into a stall where Dusty had strewn a fresh bed of hay. Using Drew's jargon, he asked, "Wanna play licky-face?"

A mind-shattering kiss answered his question. Suddenly they were locked in a passionate embrace, the passion that they'd been keeping banked burst into flames that instantly consumed them.

Joshua's hands were everywhere at once, on her face, her throat, her breasts, her waist, tugging her leg over his hip until his thigh nestled strongly against her. The sweet-smelling hay was an aphrodisiac no one could have duplicated; it prickled their skin and enveloped them in its softness.

And that was how Drew found them.

His young eyes went wide with shock. Automatically he covered his mouth with his hand to keep from making a sound.

His father loved Kristine! He didn't love him!

"You bastard! You gonna love her and leave her like you did my mom!" He swiped at the tears that were streaming down his face. Yanking Misty Blue's reins from a hook, he ran down the corridor, pulling the horse after him. "I hate you! I'll always hate you!"

Joshua got to his feet and sprinted after him, tucking in his shirttail as he went. "Drew! Stop! Damn it, don't you get on that horse!"

"I don't have to do anything you say! I hate you!" Drew jumped on Misty Blue's back. Kicking her flanks, he shouted, "Giddyap! Go, horse!"

Joshua followed for a moment. Then, realizing he'd never catch them on foot, he made a beeline for the Cherokee. He had to stop them before they got to the highway!

Standing in the barn door, dazed by how quickly everything had happened, Kristie couldn't think of anything to do but yell, "Drew! You don't understand! Come back here!"

She'd trained Misty Blue to come to her when she put two fingers in her mouth and whistled, but she was afraid that if she did her horse would stop abruptly and throw Drew over her head. Paralyzed with fear, she could only stand there and watch Drew flopping in the saddle as he charged up the lane.

It had been months since she'd ridden Misty near the highway. With an inexperienced rider in the saddle, she didn't know how the horse would react when cars speeding by at fifty miles an hour caused blasts of hot wind to buffet her.

She heard the roar of the Cherokee. Her gaze moved from Drew to the black vehicle, which was spewing sand as it grabbed for traction, and back to the horse and rider. Her first reaction was to run after Joshua, to make him take her with him. But she knew she'd just be wasting precious seconds.

Her gut twisted into a knot when she measured the distance between Drew and Joshua, and the distance between them and the highway.

"Oh, my God!"

The flag was up on the mailbox! A long, sleek Lincoln was turning into the lane. The driver must have seen Drew, but instead of slowing down and waiting the car accelerated.

"No!" she cried, reaching out as though she could stop the inevitable. "No! No!"

It was as though her mind had become a slow-motion camera. She watched as Misty Blue's front legs extended to jump the drainage ditch. Drew's feet flew out of the stirrups as the horse lunged. His bottom raised off the saddle, and then he crashed down on the horse's haunches. He slipped to one side as Misty Blue struggled to get a footing in the loose sand. Then the horse reared and threw Drew high in the air, as if he were a rag doll.

Kristie covered her ears; her fingers dug into her scalp. It might have been her anguished scream she heard, or Drew's, or Joshua's. Her head seemed to explode with sound.

Drew landed on his back, bounced once, then lay stock-still.

Medicine bag. Get your medicine bag! Kristine's training took over as she ran for her car. Keys! In her purse. In the bedroom. Get a blanket. She bolted through the kitchen, knocking a chair aside, not bothering to right it. Within seconds she was in her bedroom, ripping the coverlet off her bed with one hand and grabbing her purse with the other.

Every minute, every second, was precious to the victim of an accident. Only the thought of Joshua being with Drew allowed her to remain remotely rational. He'd know not to move him. Head or back injuries could be complicated by someone acting imprudently.

It seemed to take her forever to get back through the house, get in her car, fit the key into the ignition and get to the scene of the accident. In reality it took less than five minutes.

Drew's grandparents were standing beside their car, holding on to each other, crying softly. Joshua was hunched over Drew as though he were protecting him with his own body.

"Don't come near him," she heard him grind out between clenched teeth. "Stay away, damn it. He's going to be okay. Everybody just keep back." His massive shoulders shook as he murmured. "Drew, oh my God, son, what have I done to you?"

Kristie approached him cautiously. His eyes were wild, tormented; his skin was white beneath his tan. He was a father protecting his young from further injury. It was a potentially explosive situation.

"Joshua..." Her voice held a strange calmness. "Sit back. Let me help Drew."

"You've done enough damage. Drew wouldn't be here if it weren't for you and his grandparents. I could have gotten to him before he reached the highway."

Inwardly she flinched, but she suppressed her guilt feelings. She could deal with them later. Now the injured child was her first priority.

She knelt beside Drew's legs. Starting at his ankles, she checked swiftly for broken bones. As she worked her way up his body, she covered him with the blanket she'd brought to lower the risk of his going into shock.

She silently blasted Joshua. Move!

She nudged him with her arm until she could reach Drew's wrist. His pulse was accelerated, but strong. His hands were clammy with sweat and grit. His fingers curled around her thumb. A good sign.

"I think he may have just had the wind knocked out of him." She pulled her stethoscope from her medical bag. "I want to listen to his chest, check the pupils of his eyes, make certain there's no neck or head injury. You can stay close, Joshua, protect him, but you've got to give me some room."

Joshua convulsively hunkered lower. His knees dug into the sand on one side of Drew, and his elbow dented the ground on the other side. "No."

"Look at me, Joshua."

His head jerked toward her. Their eyes met—his filled with helplessness and guilt, hers with confidence and determination.

"You're going to have to trust me. Now." Her voice was hushed, but it rang with authority, and it conveyed a sense of the urgency of the situation. "I care for Drew. I won't hurt him. Trust me."

The fierceness in his eyes faded, and his face crumpled. The tears he'd been holding in check started to flow. Defeated, knowing that his stubbornness was doing more harm than good, he rocked back on his haunches.

"Don't let anything happen to him," he whispered raggedly. "I'll die if it does."

She nodded. Skillfully she finished running her hands over Drew. His face was flushed. A purplish-blue knot had formed at his hairline. He'd hit his head. That would account for his brief unconsciousness. She could smell orange Kool-Aid on his breath when she raised his eyelids. The pupils contracted normally. No concussion.

"Sorry, Kristie," Drew whispered. His eyelids fluttered open. Tears slid from the corners of his eyes. "Don't be mad. I didn't mean it."

Almost certain he hadn't sustained any broken bones or other major injuries, she said, "I know, Drew. I'm not angry with you. Can you sit up?"

She supported his shoulders; his arm draped around hers as he buried his face in her chest.

"I hate him." He sucked air into his lungs in sharp gasps. "I hate them all. They say they love me, but they just want to quarrel and bicker..."

"C'mon, sweetheart. Let me help you to the car and get you to the house. You'll feel better once I've washed the grime off of you."

"You won't let them grab at me, will you?" He sniffled and dug his fists into his eye socket. "I have nightmares about them cuttin' me in half and each takin' their share."

Kristie heard Joshua moan softly behind her. As she helped Drew to his feet, she glanced at him. His fists clenched and unclenched. His jaw worked, but he did not speak.

She wanted desperately to help him. He plainly wanted to say something, something that seemed to be wedged in his throat, behind a wall of tears. Half supporting Drew, she moved toward her car. Joshua followed mutely, looking like the walking dead.

The Van Horns started to close in on them before they reached the ditch. Drew's grandmother was leaning heavily on her husband's arm; he was leaning on an ebony cane.

When Drew saw them, he wrapped his arms around Kristie's waist and muttered, "Make them go away. Please. I've caused enough trouble."

"You heard him. He's taken a hard fall, and he's shaken up, but he'll be okay." Her eyes were blazing when they moved from Drew's grandparents to his father. "You were lucky this time. Are you people blind? Can't you see you're smothering him with your love? For Drew's sake, settle your differences, once and for all! I'm taking him back to the house."

She helped Drew across the ditch and into her car. Carefully she backed the car down the lane until she reached an entry into the side pasture where she could turn around. Her last glance up the lane left her feeling wretched. The drainage ditch might as well have been the Mason-Dixon line. Neither Joshua nor the Van Horns had crossed it. They were simply staring at each other.

Drew touched the side of her face with the back of his hand. "You love Dad, don't you?"

"Yeah, but right now I don't like him very much. He's hardheaded, proud—" Drew's hands dropped to the dashboard. Drew was angry, too, but he was also as defensive about his father as she was about Carlton, she realized. "And sensitive and compassionate. And he loves you."

Drew's brow puckered.

"Headache?"

"Only where the lump is."

When she'd parked the car by the kitchen entry, Drew turned to her and asked, "Why didn't you tell me he loves you?"

"Maybe it was because he expected you to be upset."

"Or maybe he started loving you and quit caring about me?" A fresh batch of tears threatened to cascade down his face. He blinked furiously to keep them behind his eyelids. "I don't blame him. I shout 'I hate you' when I'm feeling...like nobody loves me. It's like—" He paused to wipe his nose on his sleeve. "It's like if I do something bad...real bad...everybody notices me."

Kristie slid her arm around his shoulders and hugged him. "We all do that, sweetheart. At your age it's called teenage rebellion. At my age we don't yell 'I hate you,' but we do things we know will irritate people and make them notice us. It's called passive resistance."

Drew mulled over-that for a moment, then asked, "Like you and Dusty saddling up Whiskey for Dad to ride?"

"Yeah, something like that." She brushed his hair away from his brow and planted a kiss there. "You've rubbed sand around your eyes until you look like a raccoon. C'mon. Let's go inside and get you cleaned up. You need to soak in a hot tub or your bones are going to be awful sore tomorrow."

Before they entered the kitchen, Kristie paused to see what was going on at the end of the lane. Mr. Van Horn was shaking his cane in Joshua's direction; Joshua was shaking his head.

"They're fighting," Drew said, sighing. "They always fight. They must have been real stinkers in first grade."

Not following his line of thinking, Kristie asked, "What makes you say that?"

"You're supposed to learn to share in first grade."

She put her knuckle under his chin and lifted his head. "In that case, we all should have flunked."

"Uh-uh!" Drew said. "I can share Dad with you. I just don't want to be left out."

"I'm in touch with that emotion. I've felt shut out. I won't let that happen to you, Drew."

She led him through the kitchen to the guest suite. While she ran hot water into the tub, Drew undressed and put on his robe. Remembering how modest she'd been at his age, she offered to fix him some lemonade and excused herself.

Twenty minutes later she carried a pitcher of lemonade and two glasses into his room. Drew was in his pajamas in bed. He stared at the ceiling as though he thought he could find the solution to his problems there.

The sound of ice clinking against the side of the pitcher broke his deep concentration. He sat up and leaned back against the headboard. Kristie poured him a glass. He took it, swirled the ice cubes around with his finger, then licked it.

"Feeling better?" Kristie inquired, sitting on the edge of the bed examining the colorful Easter egg on his forehead.

"I know how the chicken feels when Maude shakes it in a brown paper bag before she cooks it," he told her. He sipped his lemonade, staring at Kristie all the while.

Something was obviously bothering him, but Kristie decided to wait until he felt enough at ease to talk about it.

"Kristie?"

"Ummm?"

"Suppose you and Dad got married. And suppose you had a baby." He blushed, but he had the courage to continue. "Would you and Dad love your baby more than you loved me?"

"No," she answered simply.

"How come?"

"Because the four of us would be family. It wouldn't be your dad's baby, or my baby, or your baby. It would be *our* baby, part of the family."

"Would you love Dad more than you loved me?"

"I'd love both of you, but differently."

"The same, but different? That sounds like a riddle, but I know what you mean. I love Dad and I love Grandfather and Grandmother, but I love them differently. And I love you and Jenny Lynn, but differently. I like it when you hug me, but it doesn't make my stomach feel mushy inside, like when Jenny holds my hand.''

Kristie returned her glass to the tray on the night-stand. ''Drew, you and your dad are a family. I'm the outsider who wants to be loved. It's as important to me that you want me as your mother as it is that your father want me for his wife. Both of you have to let me be a part of your family.''

''No one is going to be excluded,'' Joshua said from the hallway. ''Drew, your grandparents are in the kitchen waiting to see you.''

Kristie wondered how long he'd been listening.

''They are?'' Drew kicked back the coverlet and swung his legs off the edge of the bed. ''You aren't mad at them?''

Joshua shook his head and crossed to the bed. He knelt down between Kristie and Drew. ''Grown-ups make mistakes, son. I've made my share. I thought I was doing the right thing by keeping them away from you, by not telling you how I felt about Kristie.'' He lifted Kristie's slender hand to his mouth, then sand-wiched it between his and Drew's. ''Unintentionally I was doing the same thing to Drew that Carlton had done to you—I excluded him. More than anything, I want us to be a family. What do you think, Drew?''

Drew was grinning from ear to ear. ''You can ask her to be your wife and I can ask her to be my mother! What do you think?''

''I think that's the smartest idea I've heard in a long time,'' Joshua answered. He lightly squeezed both their hands. ''Kristie, would you do me the honor of be-coming my wife?''

''And would you do me the honor of becoming my mom?''

Tears of happiness made Kristie's eyes shine brightly. "Yes and yes. When?"

"Today!" Drew hugged them both.

Joshua chuckled. "We'll have to pick out a ring and get a license first."

"Can we invite Grandmother and Grandfather? Won't they be part of the family, too?"

"And Carlton? And Maude and Dusty?" Kristie asked.

Drew chimed in: "And the aunts and uncles and nieces and nephews and cousins?" Not waiting for an answer, he scooted off the bed and hurried through the door. "We're gonna have a superhumongous family!"

Kristie's eyes sparkled with happiness. "My future son recovers quickly, doesn't he?"

"You're good medicine for all of us." He kissed her fingertips. "Should I have waited to propose? In the movies there's always a cozy dinner for two with soft music and champagne."

She curled her arm around his neck and drew his face to her chest. "This is real life, Joshua. Besides, what could be more romantic than having the two men in my life ask me to be their very special woman?"

"You are a special lady." He lifted his head; his almost-dimple sank deep into his cheek as he gave her a heart-stopping smile. "I love you, Dr. Kristine Fairbanks. I love how you make me laugh when I don't want to. I love how you set me on fire with one tiny glance. I love how we fit together as though we were designed for each other. But, most of all, I love how you love me...and Drew...and every patient who walks into the clinic. I swear, I'll do everything within my power to make you happy."

Her arms tightened around his neck as she slid off the bed and onto her knees. "You already have, love. You already have."

Ten

"Quit fussin' with your veil, Kristie. I've got enough bobby pins in the crown of your hair to hold down the Goodyear blimp!"

"I'm a little nervous." That was the understatement of the century, Kristie mused, smiling weakly at her image in the full-length mirror. Then, more truthfully, she said, "I'm a *lot* nervous."

From the dressing room, which was near the front doors of the church, she could hear the surprised reactions of the wedding guests as they entered and heard the popular music the organist was playing.

This wasn't going to be the ordinary get-the-vows-exchanged-and-rush-to-the-reception wedding; it was going to be extraordinary. At least that was what she'd thought when they'd planned it. Now she worried about their friends wondering if she was playing the game of life with a full deck!

"Are the men here?"

"Dusty has them corralled in the minister's office. Stop fretting! You look lovely." Maude's hands trembled as she tugged at the jacket of her lavender silk suit. "Your matron of honor may collapse halfway up the aisle, but you can just step over me and carry on with the wedding."

Juliet Van Horn edged closer to Maude. Dressed in a pastel pink silk that matched Maude's in cut and style, she appeared elegant, but her gloved hands were trembled, too.

"I walk up the aisle ahead of you, Maude. You'll have to step over me!"

Jenny Lynn, who'd been peeking through the door, twirled around in her younger version of the older women's suits. Holding a basket filled to the brim with rose petals up high, she said, "That's okay. If you fall you'll land in a bed of roses!"

"That's a comforting thought," Maude said, grinning. "One thing about it, though…with all the doctors from the clinics being the ushers, we won't have to worry about there being a doctor in the church!"

"Oh!" Jenny Lynn squealed. "It's time! Here comes Drew's new grandfather."

Kristie took one last deep breath and fingered the string of matching pearls Joshua had given her as a wedding gift. With her hair piled in ringlets beneath the veil and the flush of anticipation painting her cheeks the hue of ripe apricots, she knew she'd never looked better. The simple, classic style of her ivory silk suit flattered her figure. But, just in case she wasn't as beautiful or as poised as she wanted to be, she rubbed her toe on the borrowed penny Drew had told her to put in her slipper for good luck. As she crossed to the door she could feel her satin blue garter caressing her legs.

Something old, something new, something borrowed and something blue—the whole family had insisted on following a few of the traditions.

Maude and Juliet each gave her a peck on the cheek before they left the room to line up at the end of the church aisle. Carlton, looking tanned and fit from his weeks in the Bahamas, crooked his arm and beamed at her radiantly.

"You look as beautiful as your mother did on our wedding day," he said, every inch the proud father. "I don't know who's the happiest man here today—Joshua, Drew or me."

She'd promised herself she wouldn't be a sentimental slob and cry at her own wedding, but the pride gleaming in her father's eyes was nearly her undoing. She bit her lip to keep her chin from wobbling as she tucked her hand in the crook of his arm.

When Juliet began her slow march up the aisle, Carlton whispered, "You love him, don't you? You aren't marrying him because of what I said, are you?"

Shaking her head, she answered simply, "I love Joshua the way you loved Mom."

She heard his breath whisper between his lips and saw a tear slide from the corner of his eye. His voice held an emotional edge when he said, "I've done a lot of thinking about you and Joshua . . . and me and Gloria. I remember calling home two or three times a day because I missed having her with me. I think—" He cleared his throat to make his voice loud enough for Kristie to hear him. "No, I envy you and Joshua working together, side by side. You'll always be there when you need each other. My only regret is not always being there for you."

She would have contradicted him, but he shook his head lightly. "I do love you, Kristine. I always have. I admit to wanting to mold you into the image of your mother, but I'm glad you're who you are. I'm proud of the woman you've grown up to be . . . a loving woman and a caring doctor. A man couldn't ask for more from his daughter."

Kristie swallowed, once, then again. Unable to speak, she tightened her fingers on Carlton's sleeve to communicate her love for him.

She'd waited so long to hear his praise, to have him see her as an individual, to see that what he'd considered her inadequacies were the foundation of her strength.

Raising on tiptoe, she brushed his cheek with her lips. "Thank you for telling me that, Dad. It's something I'll always remember, always cherish."

The organ music swelled.

Smiling genuinely now, she clutched the spray of orchids and gardenias Joshua had chosen for her and let her father lead her to her destiny. A warm glow replaced the butterflies swarming in her stomach when she saw Joshua, Drew, Dusty and William Van Horn waiting near the altar. She barely noticed the fragrance of orange blossoms permeating the air, the soft candlelight casting mellow rays on the smiling faces of their guests, the rose petals beneath her feet.

She saw only her loved ones, her family, waiting to make their vows.

When they reached the altar, Carlton gently placed her hand in Joshua's and said, "Be happy."

Joshua's fingers curled around her small hand. The smile he gave her was brighter than the Florida sun in July.

"You're beautiful," he whispered. "Truly beautiful."

The minister began the service by saying solemnly, "We are gathered here to celebrate the wedding of Kristine Fairbanks to Joshua Hayden."

In a daze, Kristie heard his voice melodiously extolling the virtues of marriage, then reading passages from the Bible. But her thoughts were on the vows they'd be exchanging, and hers in particular.

She and Joshua and Drew had spent hours clustered around the kitchen table discussing what this marriage meant to each of them, individually and as members of the family. And then they'd gone their separate ways to write what they'd say at the wedding.

Lost in her daydream, she started when Joshua raised her hand to the front of his tuxedo and held it there. Beneath it she could feel the steady beating of his heart as he spoke. His eyes drew her into their dark centers until she had the sensation of drowning in them.

"I, Joshua Alden Hayden, promise to love you, Kristine. Freely. From this day forward, you'll be a part of me, a part of my hopes and dreams. Each beat of my heart will be in recognition of our love. I put my love in your capable hands, knowing you'll cherish it with the same love and devotion that I'll have for you. Kristine, I'll be your friend and your lover—beyond death, when only our souls can entwine."

His solemn vows were spoken to her, but his voice carried clearly throughout the congregation. She was totally unaware of the collective sigh from her friends.

She was aware only of Joshua, the right man, in the right place, speaking his wedding vows.

With one hand still on his heart, she placed his hand in the valley between her pulse point and her shoulder, against the pearls he'd given her.

She spoke from her heart, softly, but with deepest sincerity. "And I, Kristine Marie Fairbanks, vow to make a home for you, Joshua Alden Hayden. I'll fill it with our loved ones and decorate it with love. You'll never feel alone or lonely. I trust and respect you. I'll be there to laugh with you during the good times, and we'll lean on each other to cry should there be difficult times. I truly hope the joyous love I feel for you will guide us and protect us. I love you, Joshua, here and now and to eternity."

For a long moment, their eyes held.

"Do you have the rings, Drew?" Joshua asked, turning to his son.

There were tears in Drew's eyes when he reached into his pants pocket and placed three gold bands in his father's hand.

While Kristie held Drew's hand, his father slipped the smallest ring on his son's smallest finger. "This ring makes you a part of both of us."

"It's symbolic of the circle of love that will surround you," Kristie added.

In unison, they said, "We'll both nourish you with a wealth of love, until death do us part."

Drew proudly lifted his eyes from the ring to both their faces. "I, Drew Hayden, do solemnly promise to grow up to be the best that I can be, because your love will make me big and strong. And, if our family grows, our love will grow until there's plenty for all of us. I love you, Dad. You, too, Mom. Forever and ever."

Kristie felt her heart thudding in her chest as Joshua slid the next-smallest ring on her fourth finger. He lifted her hand to his lips and kissed the ring and her finger as though his life's breath would seal the ring permanently in place. "With this ring I thee wed, my love."

Choked with emotion, Kristie thought it would be a miracle if she could say anything else. It took several moments before she could pick up the largest ring and slide it on Joshua's finger. "With this ring I thee wed, my love." She kissed her husband's ring, and then Drew's. "We are man, wife and son."

Joshua hugged his son and kissed his bride.

Drew recovered his wits before either his mom or his dad. He reached into his other pocket and pulled out five rings. The seven tiny diamonds set in gold in each ring twinkled brilliantly in the candlelight.

Proudly he turned to the other members of his family. One by one he placed rings on his grandparents' fingers, then on Maude's, Dusty's and Carlton's. As he slid each ring into place he said, "This is a token of our love and esteem, because you are part of our family."

None of them had expected to be included in the exchange of rings. There wasn't a dry eye among the five of them when Kristie kissed each of them on the cheek and Joshua did the same.

The minister raised his hands. "I now pronounce you man and wife. You may kiss the bride."

The minister paused. He'd seen hundreds of weddings, all of them beautiful, all of them with the bride and groom vowing undying love, but none of them had touched him the way this one had. His chin quivered as he uttered the final words of the ceremony, "And I

pronounce you . . . united as a family. May you all live happily on God's earth and beyond, in His kingdom.''
   And they did.

*   *   *   *   *